You Can't Bring Them Back

Matthew Yoppini

Julia Wisner

Illustrator

Part 1: The Valley of Monkeys

      Excalibur is leaving home tonight, he is fourteen. He's putting his boots on as quickly as he can. He stayed up and pretended to fall asleep when his parents went to bed; he has to be quiet and move quickly because they are coming to take him. His parents called them on him. He puts on his big red coat and packs a few essentials into his pink backpack. He opens the door and looks out into the blistering cold of the winter night. He looks at the pure snow illuminated by their porch light and shivers. He looks back into the house one last time, a few snowflakes fly in.

      His boot crunches the snow beneath his foot as he steps into the night. He slowly closes the door behind him. Upstairs, his mom turns over in her sleep. A few hours pass and the men from the camp knock on the front door then go into Excaliburs room to find an empty bed. The neighborhood is swept and they send large men with guns to his friend's house. They don't find him because during that time he's boarded a long-distance bus heading East.

      Looking out the window of the bus he watches the city lights grow more distant soon the vast expanses of urbanization are replaced by hills and mountains. The wind is howling and his mother is sobbing as his father pats her on the back. Excalibur falls asleep on the bus. Stopped at a gas station high in the mountains he wakes up, the driver is shaking him demanding to see his ticket; he pretends to look for it, knowing he won't find it because he's snuck onto the bus. Without a ticket or money to pay for one, he's kicked off and left there. He watches the bus drive away, and flips it off yelling, "Fuck you!" while he throws his bag in its general direction.

A few minutes later, Exalibur wipes the frozen tears from his face and picks his bag off the road before someone runs it over. He sits at the bus stop, thinking and rubbing his arms to keep himself warm. He goes inside and looks at the long johns; he flips over the tag, looks at the price, he looks to his left then to his right before ripping the long johns off the rack and running out. The manager chases after him, but Excalibur is already around the mountain bend, catching his breath.

He walks a mile down the road, holding his thumb out to passing cars. He goes another mile or so until he finds an overpass where he can change into his long johns without getting arrested for public nudity. Throwing off his jacket and kicking his boots off as quickly as he can, he's shivering. After completely disrobing, he jumps into his long johns, and dresses again. Cars are driving above him, a semi drives on the overpass, its massive engine sends deafening echoes off the mountain wall and into the nook beneath the overpass where he's changing. Loose snow falls down and is swept toward Excalibur. He nearly slips, but catches his fall on what he thinks is a rock.

He looks to his left and sees that he's not holding onto a rock, but the shoulder of a homeless man frozen into the wall. The homeless man is sitting down, his eyes are closed and his arms are crossed. Excalibur steadies himself and looks at the man, "Shit poor dude," he says as he wipes his hand on his pant legs. He climbs out of the overpass and takes out his phone to call the police. He tells them where the body is and leaves the scene because he assumes that he's been reported missing and the police will ask for his name. The truth is that his parents haven't reported him missing and they won't, they don't care if he lives or dies.

Excalibur walks until the sun begins to set. He spends the night in an abandoned cafe. The windows are boarded and the floor creaks as he walks on it. Echoes of the past live in the cafe, Excalibur is squinting his eyes he can almost see people still sitting on the stools that surround a bar. They're wearing old-fashioned clothes and reading newspapers before going to their jobs. In one booth he can see the faint outline of an old woman with her hands resting on the table. He wonders why she's sitting by herself. When he steps closer, her echo disappears.

In the back of the cafe he finds an old cot and a few non-perishables that were left behind. It looks like whoever used to own the cafe left in a hurry because there are still cups and a few bags of coffee beans under the counter. Excalibur takes a cup out and wipes the dust out with his shirt then turns on the faucet not expecting it to work but it does. He picks up one bag and looks at the expiration date. It's two months from now. He feels an icy chill pass through him and sees the shimmering outline of a woman wearing an apron.

He takes the cot outside and beats it until dust stops coming from it. He eats, drinks some water, then passes out in the cot from exhaustion. In his dreams he sees a monkey statue holding a piece of gold. The monkey statue looks at him and hands him the piece of gold. Waking up the next day with a headache, he reaches into this backpack and pulls out his medicine; he takes it with a glass of water. He takes a bag of coffee beans.

Excalibur notices something he hadn't the night before. The cash registers look like they've been pried open and emptied of their cash. Light shining through the boards on the windows show dried blood and bullet holes. The bullet holes are almost big enough for him to put his little finger in. He gently touches the bullet holes, and the dried blood, flakes of blood come out of the ceramic as he runs his finger across it. One of the cash registers is flipped laying face down on the floor right in front of the bar. He picks it up, it's heavier than he expected, there's still a few small bills inside, he pockets them.

Thirty minutes after leaving the cafe, he's picked up by a couple in a wood paneled sedan. One woman asks him what he's doing up here by himself. He tells her he went out for a hike and lost his way. The other woman who has blonde hair says, "Haven't we all… haven't we all"

The woman with black hair offers him a granola bar he tries to refuse, but she says, "Now now, it's rude to turn down a gift, isn't it?" He reluctantly takes the granola bar and puts it in his jacket pocket. After a few minutes of uncomfortable silence, the black-haired woman says, "I'm sorry we didn't get your name"

He looks at his feet and says, "My name is Excalibur"

The blonde woman says, "Excalibur, huh, well my name is Dorris and this tall drink of water with her feet up on the dash is May,"

Excalibur says, "Nice to meet you both" and looks out the window. While looking at the tall snow-covered mountains and silent hills, he notices the door is locked. "Hey you didn't ask me where I'm going" He touches the area where there should be a door handle and feels an empty space. He looks down, then looks to the other rear door, horrified he realizes the door handles have been removed. He yells, "Let me go you fuckers" and hits them with his bag.

The two women and Excalibur struggle. He punches May, giving her a bloody nose. He cuts his knuckle on one of Dorris' canines. During the fight, they drift into oncoming traffic. A red semi truck is coming around a mountain bend, the driver of the truck picks up a burger and lifts it to his mouth. Dorris scratches Excalibur's face. The driver cranks the wheel to avoid hitting them. He drops his burger causing lettuce, ketchup and other ingredients you would expect to find in a burger to be thrown all over the cabin. The semi drives through the railing, into the side of the mountain, scraping half the trailer off. Dorris drives off the mountain, and their car crashes into a tree some distance from the pass they were driving on.

The wood paneled station wagon is split in half. May is thrown from her seat through the window because she took it off to fight Excalibur. Dorris has a tree branch through her lung and glass in her face. Excalibur is bruised, beaten, and scratched, but he'll be okay. He unbuckles his seat belt, climbs over the center console and through the shattered front windshield. Dorris grabs his leg, gasps one last time and says, "May."

He sweeps the broken glass of his pants and pulls a piece of shrapnel from his shoulder. When he does this, he realizes he's missing his backpack. He looks for it around the crash site, finally finding it under May's broken body. He flips her over just enough to get his backpack, trying not to look at what's become of her. Parts of her that should be inside are outside, things are sticking out that shouldn't, most of her is missing or misplaced. He looks up at the mountain then down to the valley below and decides it would be easier to go down then try to crawl back up.

After forty-five minutes of going down the mountain, and nearly slipping multiple times, he stops to rest on a rock that looks like Abraham Lincoln. Reaching into his pocket he fishes out the granola bar May gave him then scarfs it down. He touches Abe's nose and traces the outline with his index finger. He gives The Guy On the Penny a pat on the head and keeps going until nightfall.

He sleeps in the branch of a tree, ties his belt around the branch and his waist so he doesn't fall off. In his dream he's on a distant world with three moons hanging gorgeously in the sky. Excalibur is being led by the hand by The King of The Monkeys, not the Monkey King mind you that's a different primate. The King of The Monkeys looks back to Excalibur. The King has calm, reassuring blue eyes and walks with a bamboo cane. He says, "Not far now, human boy," his voice is low and full of bass. It's calm and steady, like a brook.

Excalibur wakes in the snow below the tree he fell asleep in, his belt is carefully placed next to him. He grabs his belt and looks around fearfully before putting it on. He wipes the snow that gathered on him while he slumbered, shaking it out of his hair and clothes. His stomach is roaring, and he's freezing, so he finds a cave to eat cans of beans and corn in. Sitting at the edge of the cave eating, he sees a gentle three eyed doe walk by. She lowers her head and eats a poppy sticking out of the snow. The three eyed doe looks at Excalibur and blinks her two normal eyes, then blinks her third eye. She opens her mouth like she's about to say something and then decides not to. Maybe she realized that a talking three eyed deer would frighten a young boy.

The doe cautiously approaches Excalibur; she lowers her head and allows him to pet her. He strokes her head and pats her legs. Her three eyes are even more stunning up close, her long eyelashes make them even more beautiful. When he finishes petting her, she bows to him then walks back into the woods to eat more flowers. In a tree just out of his sight a macaque is watching. Excalibur finishes eating and leaves the cave. The macaque gets stays of sight by climbing higher, but he's still watching.

The mountains surrounding Excalibur seem further than anything; it seems like it would be more possible to reach out and grab a star from the sky than reach the mountain top. As he makes his way further into the valley, the snow becomes less heavy, and he can see the ground. He finds a small statue made of sticks that resembles a gorilla on a rock with a smooth top, it's crude in construction and no adhesive was used, just a bunch of sticks bent together to form a facsimile of a gorilla. He gently sets down the gorilla statue on the rock it was on exactly where he found it. The macaque watching him eats a handful of nuts.

Excalibur walks until the snow is behind him and there's green lush grass in front of him. He finds a patch of poppies and lays in it while looking up at the fluffy mid day clouds. He sees one that sort looks like Kim Il sung, and another that looks exactly like cotton candy. A plane flies low overhead, there's a man with a big camera sitting where the door opens taking pictures of the valley. He looks right at Excalibur laying in the poppy patch and takes a picture.

The photographer makes a circular motion with his hand. The pilot turns the plane; the photographer points down at Excalibur who is now sitting up to look at the plane; the pilot looks down at the boy in amazement and wonder. Questions fill his head about how he survived and how he got there. Distracted and amazed, the pilot crashes the plane into a tree. Its propeller shreds the branches and foliage, but its powerful body stops the plane's momentum. The fight is too much for the tree and goes down with the evil machine. The pilot dies almost instantly, but the photographer is pinned under one of the plane's flaming wings.

An orangutan comes from a garden where she was making a flower crown for a lady she loves. The orangutan looks at the photographer and the photographer looks up at the great ape. The man yells, "Please help" the great ape picks up a rock and hits the man until his head is a mushy pile of goo then goes back to making a flower crown. Excalibur sees this all, the tree falls over, and catches on fire, black smoke rises into the sky.

The tree, the plane, and the men who were in that plane turn to ash as the fire's roar turns into a whisper before silencing itself. The orangutan finishes her love's flower crown while watching the fire. When the fire burns itself out, Excalibur walks over and gets on his knees to say a prayer from the men who died.

The grass seems to grow greener as he walks deeper into the valley and the flowers become more frequent. He reaches The Meadow of Souls, Excalibur doesn't know this but that's where he is, it is a sacred place that few are permitted to tread. Loud screaming and growls disturb the peace and tranquility of the meadow. Excalibur looks behind him and sees that the orangutan that killed the man trapped under the wing is being forbid entry by gorillas holding spears. The orangutan attempts to push past them, holding the flower crown above her head so it isn't damaged. The apes are arguing, what they're saying is unclear. The gorillas push the orangutan back; she makes a gesture and points at the flower crown then hands it to one gorilla; he takes it and makes a different gesture that seems to suggest he understands her request and accepts. The orangutan leaves peacefully and sits where Excalibur was sitting when he watched the plane crash.

Excalibur gently touches the flowers in The Meadow of Souls as he walks through. There are small circles where the grass and flowers have been carefully cleared. In the center of the circles are different objects. In one circle there is a flat stone with a red marking on it, the marking is two horizontal lines with another line going through them at an angle. It looks like it was painted with a finger. In another of the circular clearings there is a bottle of pineapple Faygo. One of the clearing has a Little Miss

Echo doll, half of the doll's face missing, but she still has a vacant look and a blue eye. Excalibur turns the bow she's wearing to the right, Little Miss Echo says, "You're my friend I love you" her once white dress is now filthy.

The Meadow of Souls ends where the valley narrows, in a tree right in front of the place where the valley narrows, sits a black macaque who's staring at Excalibur. They're staring at each other now. The macaque makes an inviting gesture and Excalibur bows to him, then walks deeper into the valley, leaving The Meadow of Souls the way he found it. There are houses made of sticks and a network of bridges built into the sides of the mountains, far too high for any human to reach, and they don't look like humans made them. Excalibur looks up at one of the bridges connecting two houses and sees that it's tied together with vines. There's a chimpanzee eating a mango with its feet hanging off the edge of one of these bridges. When he finishes the mango he grips the pit, climbs down the mountainside with style and grace, digs a small hole, throws the pit into the hole, then buries the mango.

There are fruit trees throughout the valley, some are just saplings, some are bearing fruit, and some are just about to mature. Excalibur climbs a pear tree and finds one that's ripe; he sits on one of the branches and eats the fruit while watching a hummingbird flutter nearby. He finishes eating, puts the pit in his jacket pocket, slowly climbs down the tree, digs a small hole in the ground using both his hands and buries the pear pit. He doesn't know it, but he is being watched and has just gained a great deal of respect. A chimpanzee sitting above him jumps down and spits on the mound, puts his hands together, then spreads them to explain that trees need water to grow. Excalibur taps the side of his head to show that he understands.

The chimpanzee climbs up the side of the mountain and goes into one of the huts. A minute later he finds Excalibur who walked deeper into the valley and hands him a piece of gold. The chimpanzee gives him a big open mouth smile, Excalibur does the same expression, the chimp leaves to do his monkey business.

Excalibur walks for thirty minutes the density of the huts on the mountain sides and the number of monkeys increases. He finds a giant monkey statue that's at least twenty feet tall; it has vines growing around it, there's a pool of water in between its crossed legs, and it holds its palms out. In its palms are massive piles of gold, so much gold that its palms are overfull and the gold is running over. There's gold in the pool of water and in a circle a few feet around the statue. Excalibur takes out the piece of gold he was given and looks at it, it's shiny. He wonders if the monkey polished it, he can see his reflection in it and he doesn't like it, he wishes he had more masculine features, maybe a beard and big square jaw. He looks up at the gold filled monkey paws; he throws the gold in the air then catches it to get a feel for its weight, then he tosses it into the monkey's left paw. There's an orangutan waiting behind him, the great ape throws the piece of gold he's holding into the monkey statue's right paw.

Out of curiosity Excalibur looks behind the statue there he finds a pile of human bodies in various states of decomposition, their wardrobes are varied. One of them is a pirate's skeleton leaned up against a wall. The top of the skull looks like it was crushed. Another is a soldier's body; his uniform suggests that he fought in the second world war, there is a shoddy spear stabbed through his body. The usual sort one would expect to find looking to plunder a pile of sacred gold. There are tattered flags from various nations, but mostly they're American, British, Japanese, Chinese, and Russian flags. They know about this place, but most of them have realized that it would be a suicide mission and the optics of bombing a sacred valley would be horrible.

      He walks from behind the statue, standing in front it is an albino gorilla, she tosses a chunk of gold into the statue's left palm. When she does this, a few piece falls from the top and into the water. She bows to the statue, then turns to leave. Just before she leaves, a man flies down on an American Flag parachute, screaming joyfully. He lands in front of the statue and yells, "Holy shit I'm gonna fucking wealthy" he laughs manically as he scoops hand fulls of gold into his backpack, "I'm gonna buy a god damn island" the albino gorilla puts her hand on the man's shoulder and points at the spot he's taking the gold from suggesting he should put it back. He shouts, "Take your paws off me, you damn dirty ape!" and swats her off. The albino gorilla rubs her hand, looks at the man filling his greedy pockets with sacred treasure that he has no right to. She grabs him back by the back of the neck and shoves him toward the pool of water between the statue's crossed legs. The American screams in horror, "No no please don't I'll put it back I'm sorry!" The albino gorilla forces his head underwater. His strength is pathetic compared to hers, she holds him down as he kicks and screams. Even with the water muffling them, his screams are bone chilling. It isn't long until the struggle stops and the man is dead, his lifeless corpse relieved of the gold he tried to steal, his body is thrown onto the wretched pile.

Deeper in the valley is Monkey Tropolis, it's like New York City for monkeys. It's a holy place, Excalibur is the first human in centuries to be allowed safe entry. Here no space is wasted, in every one of the valley's diverging paths are vast fruit orchards and the mountain sides are filled to the brim with huts. It's a brilliant system that only its inhabitants truly understand, from the outside it looks like madness but it's perfectly orchestrated by the King of Monkeys.

The King lives in a hidden place in Monkey Tropolis. There is a single willow tree in front of the place where the Valley diverges into the Weeping Hollow. The thick hanging branches of the willow tree hide its entrances, but that won't hide a secret from someone curious like Excalibur. He pushes the branches of the willow tree aside and behind it is a narrow path, if he tried to spread his arms out to his sides he wouldn't be able to. After the narrow path is a grove of willow trees planted so closely together that their branches tangle. Below the trees of the Weeping Hollow there is cold and darkness, the light from the warm sun above can't penetrate the thick forestry. The monkeys have the Hallow memorized and know it well. An outsider is almost sure to get lost if they try to navigate it.

Excalibur recognizes this, so he goes through without thinking about where he's going. He walks straight until he can't, turns, then he walks straight until he can't again. He does this many times, the sun sets, making the Hallow's underside even colder. With teeth clattering and limbs shaking Excalibur says,

"Fuck this is colder than being out in the goddamn snow what the fuck" An hour later he finds a small path that has been cleared, on the ground of the path are monkey paw prints and *M&Ms*. He shines his flashlight on the *M&Ms*, a blue one hits him on the back of the head.

In a tree above Excalibur is a tarsier sloppy eating a packet of M&Ms, he's pouring them into his tiny hand then tossing them into his mouth. Excalibur shines his light on the monkey and his huge gorgeous eyes glow. This startles the tarsier, and he runs off, leaving a trail of *M&Ms* behind him. Excalibur gives chase and follows the trail of candy the monkey is dropping.

The candy trail stops, but Excalibur notices that he's been following a clear path through the thicket. One made my countless monkeys going through it over time, the equivalent of a dirt trail being smoothed by people walking over it. It's pitch black in there, and there's more life around him than he realizes. He navigates the Weeping Hollow's trail the same way one navigates a maze: he keeps going until he reaches a dead end then turns around and tries a different path; he remembers markings and unique features to avoid doubling back and getting lost the best he can. One of these features he remembers is a squirrel that looks like it's been intentionally hung, he shakes his head, "Chimpanzees" he says disapprovingly.

Eventually he reaches a pyramid. Unlike almost everything else in the valley, the pyramid is not of monkey construction but human. It's not a massive pyramid like those found in the place formerly known as Egypt, It's the size of a small house. On top of the pyramid sits The King of The Monkeys, his legs are crossed and he is glorious. He's wearing a paper hat and scrap of a red wool blanket as a scarf. In front of the pyramid are two gorillas holding sharpened sticks as spears. They stare down at Excalibur as he approaches, when he gets close they both move to the side and let him through. They're massive hulking bodies make Excalibur look like a child.

Excalibur walks up the pyramid as the sun peaks its face over the horizon, he expects it to feel old and brittle beneath his feet so he's surprised by the strength and sturdiness of the structure. He notices how well maintained it is; the pyramid is the only thing in The Hollow not completely covered with vines, and it looks like it's cleaned regularly. At the top of the pyramid Excalibur greets The King of The Monkeys, who is not to be confused with The Monkey King. The King of The Monkeys is eating a bag of *Skittles* and looking over The Hollow. Excalibur looks where he's looking and is surprised by how small The Hollow is because from the underbelly it feels massive and endless. The King offers him a skittle without looking at him Excalibur takes it and throws it in his mouth. He can't remember having a *Skittle* before, it was rare that they had candy in Excalibur's house because his parents thought candy led to immorality and sin.

The King finishes his bag of skittles then offers his paw to Excalibur who accepts it, he's led to a hidden passage. The hidden passage is behind a pile of candy wrappers and soda bottles, it's nothing more than a spot in the pyramid where a few bricks were removed. Being a small spider monkey, The King easily walks in, but Excalibur has to squeeze through and make himself as small as possible. The inside of the pyramid is just as small and cramped, it's lit by birthday candles that have been placed anywhere they'll fit, be it small nooks or altars for long dead gods.

The pyramid's interior is a spiral shape with the inner sanctum in the spiral's eye. The walls have carvings depicting battles, hunts, and moments of glory in the history of the culture that existed in this place long before the monkeys inhabited it. The inside of the pyramid is sweltering except for a few cold spots where Excalibur feels like his skin is going to jump off his body. He can hear whispers as he gets closer to the pyramid's center, it's not a language he understands or even recognizes but it sounds like they're scared. The last carving just before he reaches the center depicts human figures gathered closely together hugging each other, above them is something massive falling. Excalibur thinks, "Is that a goddamn nuke? No, it can't be right, they did not invent those until the 40s or something. Maybe a meteor, but fuck me that totally looks like a nuke" he tries not to think about it because the implications are horrifying. As hard as he might try, the implications are there and what this might mean shatters his world view.

After a horrifying existential crisis he reaches the center and The King is waiting in a sliver of illumination, he slowly turns to Excalibur and points to a pit in the middle of the small room. Excalibur looks down and sees no bottom, but he can hear running water. He shines his flashlight into the pit and looks down; The King pushes him. He falls for thirty seconds before sinking into a cold pool of water; the water is so cold it feels like he's being stabbed. He swims until he reaches the surface when his head is out of the water he gasps for air. He swims to the only source of light in the cave; he steps out of the water, he's shivering, and his teeth are clattering.

The King climbs down the pit then using vines hanging from the ceiling to avoid falling in the water. He gestures at Excalibur in a way that suggests he follows. Excalibur does this, The King leads him to a ten-foot pedestal. On top of the pedestal is an ancient goblet above the goblet is a blue rose covered vine, the end of the vine is right above the goblet and is slowly dripping water into the cup. The only sound in the cave is the gentle running of water and the slow trickle of water into the goblet.

The King balances his bamboo cane in front of the pedestal then jumps on top of it. Balancing on his cane, The King carefully removes the goblet from its pedestal, making sure not to disturb the holy vine. He hands the goblet to Excalibur it's carved from stone and much heavier than he expected he needs to hold it with two hands. The King makes the gesture for drinking, Excalibur looks over the cup and the standing water that's been filling it. He lifts the cup to his nose and smells it; it smells earthy and metallic. He thinks, "Fuck it I have nothing to lose and I don't want to piss off this king monkey" he drinks from the goblet, at first only a cautious sip, the water is delicious, it's slightly sweet and salty like a handful of trail mix.

When Excalibur finishes the water, The King holds out his hands and waits for Excalibur to hand him the goblet back when he does The King carefully places it back where it was. The dripping vine begins refilling it again, the light dripping sound of the water into the stone goblet is pleasant. The King gracefully dismounts his cane, and looks Excalibur in the eyes, there's a spark that wasn't there before and it looks like his eyes could catch fire any moment. The King hits Excalibur's leg with his cane then runs off; he scales the wall, swings across the ceiling vines and leaves the same way he came in. Excalibur tries to catch him but The King is too fast, Excalibur yells, "What the fuck you're just going to leave me here!" The King has already left.

Excalibur tries to climb the cave wall but falls, he shines his flashlight around the cave looking for another exit but there isn't one. He thinks that there might be a way out through the cave's pool, there is, it flows into a river. Excalibur doesn't try this because the water is too cold and he knows he would probably drown. His body would float down the river and there would be nobody to put coins on his eyes before he left the world behind.

He shines his flashlight against the glistening cave wall, while looking for a way up he notices there's small ledges on the walls just big enough for his feet. He tries to climb them but keeps slipping; he looks down at his boots, up at the wall, then at his boots again. He takes off his boots and socks, then puts them at the bottom of his backpack so they don't dirty everything else in his pack. He reaches the highest edge he can comfortably reach and slips his fingers across it, then puts his bare foot on the nearest edge. He tries to climb higher but loses grip and falls into the water.

Excalibur swims out of the water and looks at his hands and feet, he thinks, "Fuck me this shit is way too slippery I need some grit, he looks around the cave for a bit and finds some loose sediment. He uses a flat sharp stone to break it up until it's a powder, after this he finds a climbable wall that has vines near it. He rubs his hands and feet into the dirt, then starts climbing, with the assistance of the dry dirt on his hand and feet adding some much needed grip climbing the wall is a breeze.

He rests for a moment before swinging on the vines; he rests his toes and fingers on edges of the cave wall. He reaches for the nearest vine and tugs on it to feel if it has any give. It doesn't, it's growing from above through the cave ceiling, its vines are knotted and twisting, it could hold the weight of a utility truck. He swings from vine to vine then climbs up the pit. Climbing up the pit is much easier than climbing the cave wall because it's much dryer and he can see what he's doing. He doesn't have to feel for edges and finger pockets. It isn't long before he's back in the center of the pyramid.

He rolls onto his back and takes deep, exhausted breaths. He was expecting The King to be waiting for him, but he left the pyramid a while ago. The only thing he left behind is an empty skittles wrapper. Excalibur leaves the pyramid the same way he came back in. When he gets out of the pyramid, he goes back to the top of it and looks for the King. He thinks, "I'm going to give that little shit a piece of my mind" a mango pit hits him on the head. He yells, "Motherfucker" and looks up, The King is sitting on a tree branch smiling and waving at him.

The King holds up a pear, gestures to Excalibur in a way that suggests he should climb the tree and join him. The tree The King is sitting on is much harder to climb than the pear tree Excalibur climbed before its branches are farther apart and there aren't as many limbs. The first branch is ten feet from the ground so Excalibur jumps from the pyramid to it, he nearly misses but catches it and lifts himself onto the branch. The King is staring at him with bored disinterest. Climbing the rest of the way is difficult and tiring, he nearly falls a few times when he misses jumps. But he makes it, and The King scoots over so Excalibur can sit next to him. The King hands him the pear and Excalibur ferociously devours it down. The King pats him on the back and they look at The Valley from above. A soft sweet smelling breeze is blowing on their faces, the forest is gentle and calm.

Excalibur feels like he's at home, the scenery is so beautiful he feels like he could cry. From the tree top next to The King of Monkeys Excalibur can see all of The Weeping Hollow, beyond that he can see The Valley of Monkeys which goes on past his line of sight in one direction, in the other direction he can see The Meadow of Souls, he has to crane his neck and almost look behind him to see the mountain he was nearly abducted from now and the snow-covered hills he nearly died in.

A week passes and Excalibur is being trained to become a monkey warrior. He's punching his fist against the sturdy trunk of a tree, this is meant to harden his knuckles. He punches it with one fist then other, back and forth, his knuckles redden and bleed. He does this until the monkey that's training him puts her hand on his shoulder and lets him know he can stop. She's a mandrill, she has piercing yellow eyes, a bright red snout with blue lines coming from it, her nose has a long bridge that goes in-between her eyes.

Excalibur and his monkey friends sit around a fire and eat. They're making sounds at each other, but it doesn't sound angry, more conversational. A few of them know sign language, so they're talking to each other. The King would join them but he has so much monkey business to attend to that he can't make it. One of the things he's attending to is arranging something special for Excalibur. They finish eating and retire to their valley side bungalows, Excalibur hasn't mastered climbing yet, so he has a rope with many knots tied into it dangling from his hut, this was a gift from The King. Excalibur suspects The King enjoys having a friendly human around, he's right.

It's more than that though The King can see through people, meaning individuals not just humans, and understand what they're about and what they've been through. In Excalibur, The King can see significant loss and hardship. That he's never known a home or belonging. That his family abused and abandoned him, he can see the great pain that fills Excalibur. He can also see that Excalibur was born in a body that wasn't right for him, and for this he was nearly taken away in the night to an evil place that would try to fix what isn't broken in him. The King knows Excalibur needs a home and a family. Excalibur sleeps soundly in his bed, feeling for the first time that he has that.

He has a dream of fire and death. He feels like he's falling into a black cavernous pit; he falls for so long that he feels like he's flying. He looks around and sees a pinprick of light, as he moves closer toward it becomes bigger, he goes into the bright blinding light and comes out on the other end. He's in the middle of space surrounded by countless numbers of stars and they all feel like they're moving toward him. Right before he's engulfed by the flames of a million burning stars, he wakes up.

The smell of roasted mango and cooking eggs fills the air. He looks out his window and sees a chimpanzee cooking on a pan over an open flame. The chimpanzee looks up and smiles at Excalibur, the monkey points to the food, then rubs his belly and points to Excalibur who rubs his belly then points to the food. The chimpanzee slices a mango, throws it in the pan, and cracks a couple eggs in there.

Excalibur does his morning stretches, then climbs down from his bungalow. He sits across from the chimpanzee who serves him breakfast and gives him a kiss on the forehead. He's never felt more loved in his entire life. More monkeys start waking up and cooking for themselves, not all of them can start fires so they help each other out and work together using their different skills and talents. The omnivores among them even have meat for breakfast.

Aside from fruits and things they can gather from The Valley most of their goods are raided from nearby towns. Excalibur is joining them in the raid today. After breakfast he's handed a spear and given a pat on the back by an elder Orangutan. They walk out of The Valley then go through the Meadow Of Souls and take a long trail that leads to the main road. They move along the side of the road, when cars and trucks pass them they all lay as flat as they can.

One of the cars is driven by a woman, in the back seat of the car is her five-year-old son, he notices the monkeys. The five-year-old pulls his index finger out of his nose, there's a booger hanging to it, he points and yells, "Look mommy monkeys! Monkeys! I like monkeys!" he pokes the window and smears his booger on it. Without looking, she says,

"Uh huh, that's nice baby. You saw a monkey at the zoo, didn't you?"

He says, "Yea I saw lots a monkeys I saw a gorillas and chimpanzees they were funny trying to hide!"

She looks at him in her rear-view mirror and smiles, "If they have a stuffed monkey at the grocery store do you want one?" Her son giggles and squeals, she asks, "Is that a yes my sweet boy" he nods his heads. The car leaves Excalibur and his monkey family's view, they stand up and get to the edge of town as quickly as they can.

The rain begins to pour, they can see the grocery store. The bright lights from the store cut through the rain. A gorilla with a white stripe down her face is leading the charge on this raid. Her name is Boba, when she gives the signal they all run toward the store as fast they can. The town's people are used to the monkey raids and have built dedicated monkey alarms in the stores. The monkeys run through the parking lot and the monkey alarm is pushed, above the alarm a small sign reads, Break In Case Of Ape. The store goes into lockdown and shutters cover the doors and windows. Boba uses her terrific strength to lift the shutters and let her family in.

All the monkeys know what they need to get. This being his first raid, Excalibur is the designated bagger. Boba is the lookout and support, her job is to stop anyone who impedes their raid. The woman who was driving when her son spotted the monkeys yells, "What the fuck is going on!"

A cashier who is hiding behind the checkout counter says, "It's just a monkey raid they come and get stuff?"

The woman asks, "Who's the human with them?" the cashier peaks over the counter to look because they've never had a human with them before.

The cashier is shocked, "Holy shit, they have a human with them!"

The woman's five-year-old son is holding a small stuffed chimpanzee with soft black fur he runs toward Boba he's giggling and saying, "Monkey! Monkey!" His mom runs after him when he gets too close Boba slaps him so hard he's sent flying into the flower display. His mom picks him and wipes the glass off him, he's not breathing, his small fragile body is broken.

The woman is screaming and crying, she looks at Excalibur who's filling grocery bags with what he's being brought, she yells, "You're just going to allow this!"

Excalibur stops and thinks for a moment, "This is my family you better watch yourself lady or I'll kill you myself" The woman says nothing after this, mostly because she's trying to keep her five-year-old son alive. He's clutching his stuffed chimpanzee, it's covered in blood.

The monkeys finish taking what they came for and run out the door; they disappear into the fog and rain. A minute after they're gone, the police show up, the five-year-old boy is dead. His mother screams in mourning, her cries of pain ring through the mountains and The Valley. Excalibur can feel her pain. He doesn't sleep well that night, the only thing that puts him to sleep is exhaustion.

He wakes up late into the afternoon and notices something on his bedside table. It's a bottle of testosterone, Excalibur is so happy he feels like he's going to cry. He looks at the recommended dosage and takes that much with a glass of water. He knows this is a gift from The King because nobody else could have known that he needed this or that he ran out.

A couple days pass, and he's being given jumping lessons from a macaque. The first thing his teacher wants to see is how high he can jump. Excalibur can only jump a couple feet off the ground, the macaque shakes her head in disappointment and shows him how high she can jump. She jumps almost seventeen feet in the air. Excalibur tries again, this time he bends his knees as low as he can then springs up, soaring two-and-a-half feet off the ground. The macaque calls over a senior; she explains with a series of complicated gestures and noises that Excalibur is shit at jumping. The senior macaque shows him a few exercises he can do to increase his jump height, including jumping jacks and jump squats.

The junior macaque training him makes him do these exercises until his limbs give out. Shortly after his limbs give out, Excalibur takes an afternoon nap under a tree. The junior macaque is told not to go so hard on him during future jump training, the power got to her head.

The next day he's given training from The King of Monkeys himself. Excalibur meets him next to an abandoned piano that's missing keys and its front left leg, causing it to slump. The King is sitting on top of the piano and tosses him a bamboo stick when he approaches, Excalibur fails to catch it, the stick hits him in the chest then drops to floor but not before Excalibur awkwardly fumbles with it in a horrible attempt to not let it fall. He picks the stick up off the ground. The King throws his bamboo cane in front of Excalibur, making it land perfectly on one end, then jumps from the piano onto it and stares at the boy. He smacks Excalibur on the face then jumps off the cane without it falling over and lands on the piano causing a few of its remaining strings to ring.

The King balances on one leg, points at Excalibur, then points at the bamboo stick. Excalibur asks, "You want me to balance on it" The King looks confused. He gently holds Excalibur's hand and closes his eyes, The King smiles and taps his nose with his index finger. Excalibur says, "Alright man I'll give it a try" he puts his bamboo cane standing up and tries to climb it but it falls over. The King stares at him, stroking the hairs on his chin. Excalibur tries it again with the same results, then asks, "I'm I supposed to jump onto it or something?"

The King holds both his hands and focuses intently, he transmits a thought that rings in Excaliburs head with a deep booming voice, "Yes my boy.... I've heard disappointing things about your jump training. Feel free to use the piano or a rock to reach it until you can jump like we can" The King smiles at him.

Excalibur says, "What the fuck you can do that holy fucking shit that's insane. I also totally didn't expect your voice to sound like that. How is that possible?"

The King gives a humble smile then transmits this thought, "Yes my boy I'm sorry I didn't tell you this sooner but we, all the monkeys in The Valley I mean, we've all had some rather unfortunate encounters with humans. You're not like most of them you're kind and have respect for all life. Don't let this cruel world break you." Excalibur is crying, The King wipes his tears and holds his face.

Excalibur holds the bamboo stick with a new fierce determination, he puts the stick next to the piano; he climbs on the piano and uses it to step onto the stick. He's able to balance for a few seconds before falling again. He does this again, this time he's able to stand on it with one leg just a bit longer. This repeats for hours, Excalibur is busted and blue from all the falls. When The King makes him stop, he's able to balance on the stick for ten minutes before falling.

They rest an hour for lunch then get into combat training. The King holds his cane at Excalibur in the same way a swordsman holds his weapon when he's engaging an enemy. Excalibur picks up his bamboo and does the same, The King hits him in the legs then does a backflip away. Excalibur tries to swing down at The King, but he rolls out of the way and hits the boy in the back. The King jumps on his head and playfully smacks him in the face, then jumps off and balances on his cane. The King watches Excalibur for a few moments to make sure he isn't seriously injured and can keep fighting. Excalibur flails his cane at The King, every swing misses as The King easily dodges the boy's futile attacks. Realizing that Excalibur is too emotional to fight, The King hits a pressure point that instantly puts Excalibur to sleep.

He wakes up several minutes later with his head in The King's lap; The King is stroking his head and scratching his back. The King mentally transmits this, "Anger my boy, it clouds the mind. This is just training there's no need to be mad if I'm hurting you just drop your weapon and the fighting will stop. You must be as tranquil as a gentle brook, but also like the brook swift and steady, capable of cutting through a mountain." Excalibur looks up at him and smiles, The King smiles back and gives him another pat. They continue combat training this time it goes better and Excalibur improves just slightly as a monkey warrior. One afternoon of training doesn't make someone a great warrior, but he improves if by only very little.

The last training he starts is from Boba, the gorilla she teaches him how to strengthen his muscles. They lift big mighty logs on their shoulders, Boba has to crouch down while they're carrying it to the building sites to accommodate the boy. They carry the logs from the lumberyard and bring them to the new valley side bungalows this is a one-mile walk. The monkeys waste not, every single acorn from every tree they fall is planted and every stick and piece of wood is used. Even the smallest branches are cut up and used to make toothpicks. Boba is very patient with Excalibur when he needs to rest, she lets him and she gives him water. The job takes longer than it normally would have, but that's fine at the end of the day a new bungalow is being built for a friend in need and her new friend learns some life skills and strengthens his muscles.

For two years Excalibur trains, the first day of the week each week he's strengthening his fist with a sweet, kind monkey who makes sure he doesn't go too hard on himself. When he needs to stop punching the tree because he'll cause permanent damage, she'll let him know. The tree he uses forms scars in the spots where he was punching it, but it doesn't die, it's still standing.

On the second day of week each week he does jump training with the junior macaque. She struggles with the power she has over Excalibur early on, but she slowly learns what she's doing is wrong and abusive. She learns that being able to tell someone what to do doesn't make you better than them. Excalibur learns to jump higher and higher, over the course of two years he learns to jump over ten feet from a standing position. In a year or two who knows how high he'll be able to jump.

On the third day of the week, each week, he takes a break. He can use this day however he wants. Some days he reads all day while sitting under a tree, with the sweet smelling breeze of The Valley blowing on his face. Other third days he sleeps in and lazes about doing absolutely nothing, this is truly a luxury, the days he does nothing and feels no obligation to do anything are the best. There are rare third days where he plays Monkey Ball with the monkeys. This is not Monkey Ball on the GameCube. Monkey Ball is a purely recreational game, there are no points, or established teams, or even rules. Despite this are a few ways to be good at Monkey ball, one way is to take the ball to the top of a tall tree and throw it to another monkey on the ground. Another way is to throw the ball in between two branches, or kick it in between the legs of another monkey. As long as you're doing something with the ball, you're winning.

On the fourth day of the week each week he trains with the Monkey King, who trains him to fight and balance on the end of a bamboo stick. Learning to jump onto a bamboo stick and balance on it doesn't actually take him that long to learn. This part of his training with The King takes just over two months. Becoming good at fighting with a bamboo stick is what really takes up a great deal of time, in these two years he becomes a great monkey warrior. Not as good as The King that would take a lifetime of training, but he does become great. Very few humans can match his skill.

On the Fifth day of the week, each week he trains with Boba lifting heavy things across The Valley. Boba doesn't really view this as training or even exercise, to her this work and things that need to get done, she's just glad to have someone eager to help. In the span of these two years Excalibur goes from a skinny little boy to a muscular young man, and if you look closely, you can see a mustache forming. Some might call him attractive but they would be creeps because he just turned sixteen a few days ago.

A stranger comes into the valley, a soldier. Excalibur wipes the sweat from his brow while chopping down a cherry tree that stopped bearing fruit. This wood will be used for many things, nothing will go wasted, as it should be. A shadow passes overhead, it's the soldier, he's parachuting into The Valley,

Excalibur, and all the monkeys stare at him as he lands. He lands in front of the sacred gold bearing monkey statue and takes pictures of it, "Oscar Bravo to control"

"Go ahead Oscar Bravo," says the woman on the other end of the radio

The soldier looks around and says, "I've found it, and the amount of them here is more than we could have ever imagined the damn place is infested!"

"I copy we're waiting for clearance from command," says the woman

Boba puts her paw on the soldier's shoulder, he yells, "Oh shit!" and shoots her in between the eyes. Her body falls to the ground with a thump, even in death her face is still wearing a kind expression. He shot her before the fear or shock could set in. Boba's gentle eyes are relaxed. The gun shot rings throughout The Valley, the soldier doesn't know it but thousands of monkeys are running at him.

Hearing the shot, Excalibur drops what he's doing and runs toward the sound as fast he can. He sees the soldier and what he's done; he sees his friend lying dead. He's sitting in a treetop above the soldier. He breaks a branch off the tree; the soldier looks up, Excalibur jumps down and hits the American soldier once in the head, this creates a massive dent in his helmet. The soldier drops his gun. Blood pours from the helmet and down the soldier's face, he's shaking, he falls to his knees, touches his face and looks at his blood-soaked hands. He reaches out for Excalibur and grabs his pant leg; he kicks the soldier off.

The monkeys gather to see what happened, they all kick the American soldier's dead body. This horribly damages it, it's broken and mangled when they're done it's unceremoniously thrown on the putrid corpse pile behind the statue. A chimpanzee takes off his helmet and mocks him, when his helmet is removed a chunk of the soldier's brain falls out. It makes a loud, wet, sloppy sound when it hits the ground.

Boba's body is carefully lifted by her closest friends and taken to the meadow of souls. Every monkey who knew her kisses her before they lay her to rest. Those who didn't know her and that is very few stand by respectfully. A hole is dug, she is carefully lowered in, and covered with flowers. The hole is filled, and those who loved her say goodbye, on top of her grave a stuffed chimpanzee with dried blood on its fur is placed. Those who loved her reflect on her life and all she meant to them.

While the funeral is being held, the soldier's radio receives no response. When the United States military tries to locate it, they can't because it was broken while the soldier's body was kicked. They're coming as fast as they can, with them they're bringing fire and death.

Night falls on The Valley but no one sleeps an evil energy is haunting them. At midnight they come, bombs fall and destroy the homes of the monkeys. They set the trees on fire and create light which illuminates the crimes of the United States. The screams of the monkeys echo, the sound is deafening.

Those who try to escape are shot down by snipers in helicopters hovering above the valley. This isn't a war, it's a massacre despite what they might try to tell you. At the exit of The Valley where it opens into the meadow there are soldiers, stationed with massive guns they were told, "Kill anything furry that runs out," so they do. At the exit of The Valley the bodies pile up.

After hours of bombing and fire engulfing most of the life in The Valley being extinguished. Foot soldiers are sent in to murder everyone who's still alive and they do, the monkeys that are still clinging to life or hiding are riddled with bullets even as they cower in fear and hide their faces. No mercy is shown to them.

The only person who survives the massacre is Excalibur, they spare him because he is human, but he doesn't go down without a fight. The only reason they captured him without him killing any of the invaders is because he was surrounded by thirty killers.

The Valley is gone, its forests are burned and turned to ash, its buildings and culture blown to smithereens. The Weeping Hollow was burned as well, and they turned the pyramid in its heart into nothingness, there aren't two rocks stacked on each other, or two sticks leaning against one another when the United States military was done. Everyone is dead except Excalibur, he's been black bagged and thrown in the back of a humvee. He asks them, "Where are you cock sucking mother fuckers taking me?" they don't answer. Excalibur yells, "You've just made a huge mistake by letting him live. I swear to god I'll kill all of you, what you did to The Valley I'll do to your cities. The only thing that will remain of them will be a pile of rubble and smoke, and in that smoke will be a mother clutching her dead baby as she screams into the sky!" They ignore him and turn up the music they're listening to.

The humvee is driven into the back of a cargo plane, Excalibur is removed, walked up a flight of stairs into the seating area, then sat in between two soldiers. Once the plane has taken off, the hood is lifted, and a gag is put in his mouth, "We heard you talk too much," says the soldier gagging him, he has a thick southern drawl. They land on a military base a few hours later, he's taken to a soft padded room, there are stuffed animals and squishy blocks. Excalibur sits and waits with his back against the wall, he stares at the fluorescent lights and thinks about how long it's been since he was under fluorescent lights for this long. Hours pass.

A soft gentle man enters the room, the man is wearing a knitted sweater, and has a bushy beard. Standing in front of the door is a cop. He's not looking at Excalibur or the gentle man, the cop looks right above the man's head into the empty space. The cop is thinking about what he wants for dinner. The gentleman pats Excalibur and says, "Hey bud, I'm a social worker. I was sent to do an evaluation with you and get you back to your folks alright. If you cooperate this will all go swell and it'll be super easy and groovy alright? Just gives us a few minutes and we'll get everything ready for you." The social worker and the cop walk out of the room together.

Hearing that they intend to send back to his biological parents, Excalibur's heart races and sweat pours down his face.

He looks around the room for a way out. There's a vent in the ceiling, Excalibur jumps to reach it, he slips his fingers through the grate and pulls it open. He drops to the floor, footsteps grow closer, he jumps into the open vent and shimmies in just before the social worker comes back in the room. A soldier is watching this through the camera in Excalibur's room, the alarm is sounded.

The soldiers can hear him in the vents above them, he's watching them, they're his prey. He drops down and punches one of them in the throat. His partner tries to stop Excalibur, he kicks her in the neck, his incredible strength causes her neck to snap. Excalibur takes their guns and jumps back in the vents, shortly after this the bodies are discovered and they're ordered to shoot on sight. Excalibur drops into the security room, the guard yells, "Holy shit it's you, sto-" before he can finish his sentence he's shot in the head, his blood covers the cameras and the keyboard making everything gross. Without their eyes, Excalibur has just turned the odds in his favor.

Every soldier in the base is running toward the security room, dozens of them have their guns aimed at the door. What they don't know is that Excalibur is already in the vents watching them, he swings down with his legs still inside the vent shaft, guns akimbo, hanging upside down he kills them all. The white walls are soaked red, the smell of death fills the air, their blood covers the lights giving the hallway an eerie red glow. He lifts himself back into the vent, then drops feet first landing on the mound of viscera he's created. When he lands, the mound makes a meaty squishy sound.

He kills the few remaining people standing in his way and steals a motorcycle. A mile from the base, he looks back and watches the panic from the top of the hill. He stares at the base with squinted eyes and a clenched fist, under his breath he says, "You've just made a very dangerous enemy, I don't care how long it takes I will destroy The United States, all it's army men, boats, planes, trains, and cars. This I swear. You've taken everything from me, you fuckers." with these words he rides into the setting sun.

Interlude 1: The Man Sitting Next to Me

I first saw him while riding Bart from Pleasanton to San Francisco. I was on my way to a concert, looking out the window while listening to music. I didn't have a thought in my head, not an interesting one that would be worth sharing. In the reflection I saw him, it was strange that someone was sitting next to me because there was plenty of seating in the train car. I could barely see him in the window's reflection, this man was merely an after image. The only thing I could see was that he was dressed all in black. I stared out the window for the rest of the trip, when I got up to leave the man was gone.

I didn't see him for a while after that, or at least I didn't notice him. The next time I noticed him was in class, the professor was giving a lecture. I saw him out of the corner of my eye, sitting in the empty seat next to me. I looked, but he wasn't there; the person sitting two seats over thought I was looking at him; he looked at me then looked away. I tried to pay attention to the lecture, but I could see him out of the corner of my eye. He laid his dirty soot covered hands on the desk; it looked like he had been digging. He reached in his jacket pocket and took out a dead raven, then put it on top of my notes. I took a few sheets of paper towels from the classroom paper towel dispenser, wrapped the dead raven and put it in the garbage. Everyone was staring at me with wide, terrified eyes. Later that day I had to speak to the school therapist, she suggested I get more sleep, and I asked if I had been taking anything.

My grades slipped because every time I sat down to study he was sitting next to me putting dead animals on my papers. He also smelled, every time I sat down he was there and the stench of his rot came with him. I tried to see a sold out movie hoping he wouldn't be next to me if the theatre was packed, but the person who was supposed to sit next to me missed the showing. He put a dead frog with oily black skin in my popcorn.

I obsessively jogged to avoid him and even bought a standing desk. This worked, I noticed, an improvement in mental and physical health. The only times he sat next to me were during class and whenever I had to eat with my family. I got a boyfriend and an internship with the third largest biotech research facility in California.

Things were going well for a few months. One day while out on a morning jog with my boyfriend, a car nearly hit us, but I pushed my boyfriend out of the way. The driver had just gotten off a sixteen hour shift and dozed off at the wheel. I survived, but my legs were destroyed, mangled.

I can't escape him, that's why I'm recording this, so the ones I love will know why I did what I did. I'm sorry I couldn't be stronger Nick.

I can look at him, I can see him now without him disappearing. He looks even worse than I thought he would, flesh clinging to his old bones, his eyes are black and hollow.

I'm driving now, the man sitting next to me is taking dead animals out of his coat pockets and filling the car. The smell of rot is unbearable, and the car is freezing. If I go to hell when I die, it will be a mercy. I can see the end now. My heart is racing and I'm thinking about everything I could do and become. I'm trying to stop the car but the brakes aren't working, the man sitting next to me is laughing!

Part 2: Kill For Peace!

Excalibur sits on a train speeding through the Arizona desert. The sun is beating down, outside dust devils are dancing and all the critters are hiding from the heat. Excalibur is sitting comfortably in the air condition train car, sipping on ice water.

He isn't supposed to be on this train; he snuck on. When his motorcycle was about to run out of gas he pulled into the nearest town and abandoned it. He hid on the roof of the train he's in now and dropped through the ceiling. The train attendant is coming through and checking tickets, she nudges a man awake who's sitting five rows in front of him. The man takes out the ticket out of his front pocket; she stamps it and gives it back.

Excalibur looks around for anyone that looks friendly. He sees an old man sitting alone and sits next to him, he says, "Hey man, I don't have a ticket cover for me." the old man covers him with a blanket and says,

"Don't worry son, pretend you're asleep," Excalibur covers himself with the blanket and pretends to be asleep.

The attendant reaches them and says, "I'll need to see your tickets" her hand is out. The old man reaches into his jacket pocket and gives her his ticket. She asks, "Do you have his ticket" and reaches to wake him.

The old man says, "Hey don't wake the boy. It's been a long day, can I just give you the money for his ticket so you don't have to bother him."

She glares at him then with an annoyed tone of voice says, "I guess that would be alright sir," the old man hands her the six dollars and sixty-six cents for the train ticket. She gives him a fake smile and nods, she's holding back a grimace there's anger and rage behind her eyes. One of the few joys she has in this life is throwing people off the train.

The old man taps him and says, "She's gone kid." Excalibur throws the blanket off himself and gives out a sigh of relief. Excalibur shakes the old man's hand and says,

"Thanks man, you really saved my ass." Two rows behind them, a woman desperately looks for her train ticket. She's crying and begging the train attendant not to throw her off the train.

The train attendant sneers, "Sorry ma'am you know the rules" the train attendant grabs the woman by her collar and drags her to the train door. She pushes the woman off the train, the woman's beaten against the hard desert floor, her head is bleeding and her body is broken. The train attendant gathers the woman's belongs and throws them out too, then closes the train door.

Excalibur and the old man watch this, Excalibur offers his hand to be shook and says, "Hey name's Excalibur that's was some crazy shit."

The old man shakes his hand and point to himself, "Marco Thunderfist, I've seen crazier shit in my days but yea that was pretty fucked."

Excalibur leans backs and says, "I've got all day man let's hear your story."

Marco looks at Excalibur and smiles, "You have a last name?" Excalibur shakes his head. "Alright just Excalibur, well I'm a Vietnam vet. As someone who's been in war, I can tell you personally how fucked it is, pardon my-"

Excalibur casually says, "Ah, don't even fucking worry about it man."

Marco chuckles then continues his story, "Alright so war is fucked. I was drafted when I was nineteen. Most people knew this war was fucked, and that we were in the wrong for going there yea? But they needed bodies because there were too many young men dying. What does the United States Fucking Government do in their wisdom? They make a fucked and morally wrong war even more fucked.

"I remember the day we got the letter that I had been drafted. My mom had just made breakfast and sent my younger brother to get the mail. Our mailbox was painted like a cow, it was a bit tacky in a charming way. Among the usual mail was a letter from the US army saying I had to go off to war. I don't remember much after that, just a lot of crying, screaming, and panic.

"Next thing I know I'm on a plane with a new haircut and holding a gun. The kid next to me was crying and there was a guy across from me, the guy across from me volunteered for the war. He said to the crying kid, 'What's the matter youngin' you ain't lookin' forward to killing chinks for Uncle Sam' I look at the guy and tell him to go fuck himself and that he's a piece of shit. We fought and got broken up by the lieutenant. The guys who volunteered were always the worst. I can't remember what happened to that guy. I think he got blown up or fell in a punji pit or something like that.

"The worst thing I ever did was drop napalm bombs on this village in the jungle. God, that was fucking loud and you could see the fire for miles. Their screams still keep me up at night," Marco looks off into the distance for several seconds, "Anyway" he says, "There was also this fucking shit called agent orange right, it was supposed to just be a pesticide to clear the forests or something like that. You wouldn't fucking believe what it did the people it was used on, this shit was so bad the kids of the people who were exposed to it were born with birth defects. There's still places in Nam that are quarantined because they've been poisoned by agent orange.

"When I came back from the war and I use the word war loosely because what we did to those people was fucking genocide. When I came back… I thought about killing myself. I was sitting in my mom's basement with a gun in one hand and a bottle of whiskey in the other. I almost did it son, but I decided not to, ya wanna know why because I wasn't gonna be another victim of that fucking war. In that moment, I vowed to fuck the United States in everyway I could. An enemy of the state was born that day."

Marco pats Excalibur on the back and asks to hear his story. Excalibur says, "Well shit, where do I start. I never fit in man, and my parents hated me for it. They wanted me to be a perfect little girl, they put me in dresses and made me play with dolls. I hated that because I always knew I was a boy. I didn't have the words to express that as a kid I just knew I wasn't like the other boys, I still have a hard time expressing it because only recently that I had a family who accepted me.

"When I was fourteen, I left home. You know about the conversion camps right well my parents called this wacko fucking one that takes your kids away in the night. I found out that these fucking people coming so I get the fuck out of there." Excalibur goes into detail explaining how he found himself in The Valley of Monkeys and talks for a long length of time about all his friends and family. With tears in eyes, he tells Marco about how the United States Military took them from him. Marco hugs him and they cry on each other, everyone else on the train is trying not to pay attention.

Marco wipes the tears from Excalibur's eyes then asks, "So you don't have a place to stay?" Excalibur shakes his. Marco pats him on the shoulder, "Why don't you stay with me son all you need to do is a few chores here and there."

Excalibur hugs him again and shouts, "You mean it!" he's about to cry again, "That's the nicest thing another human has ever done for me." he's crying now him and Marco are hugging. Marco can't remember the last time he had a friend. They celebrate their new friendship with drinks and food. Hours later they reach the stop Marco needs to get off at, Excalibur comes with him. Marco's car is parked in the train station parking lot. It's a Volvo from the 90s with tinted black windows.

Marco lives in a farmhouse he inherited from his grandfather. He has acres of dirt, long uncut grass, and weeds. In Marco's living room is a big dusty recliner with a blanket on it, the house looks like it hasn't been cleaned in years. Marco sits down, turns on the TV, and kicks the feet of the recliner out. He gestures for Excalibur to sit on the couch, when he sits a plume of dust comes up. Marco turns the channel over to the news and says, "Watch son, it's about to happen" An emergency broadcast cuts off a rerun of Family Matters. The anchorman looks tired and disheveled.

Behind the anchorman is a tall burning building he says, "This just in, a bomb has been set off in the Tucson FBI building-" Marco mutes the channel and pours himself a drink.

Excalibur looks back and forth between the TV and Marco. Marco releases a calm, relaxed breath, "Yup, I did that and this clown can't tell you anything I don't already know, I just wanted to see the destruction. All I did was a park a van full of explosives in the garage and set a timer for about the time I was gonna get home."

Excalibur asks, "What if they found it?"

Marco laughs, "They aren't gonna bother with a normal maintenance van that's only been there for half a day."

Laying on the couch Excalibur watches with Marco, soon the building collapses in on itself. The news feed switches to the helicopter camera, the estimated death toll is in the thousands. Marco cheers and pours himself another drink. Excalibur looks at Marco's bookshelf, he fingers through the decent collection before pulling *The Hitchhiker's Guide to The Galaxy*. He reads it until Marco falls asleep. Excalibur puts a blanket over Marco and falls asleep on the couch.

The next morning he wakes early to cook and clean. The soft orange sunrise shines through the curtains as Excalibur dusts and does laundry. Marco wakes to the smell of eggs and coffee, he meanders into the kitchen and asks, "What's all this?"

Excalibur takes the eggs out of the pan, plates them, and peppers them. He says, "Oh hey man, I'm used to getting up before the sun so I figured I'd do some cleaning and make some breakfast. God, I haven't seen a fucking refrigerator in years I forgot how nice they are. You've also been so kind letting me stay here and all, so I figured I'd return the favor." Marco sits at the dining room table he can't remember the last time he saw it without a layer of dust. "How do you take your coffee man?"

In shock Marco says, "Oh um… just black is fine. I can't remember the last time someone made breakfast for me." He's smiling and his eyes are teary.

Looking outside the kitchen window into the backyard, Excalibur asks, "What's that out there covered with a tarp?"

Without looking and food in his cheeks Marco says, "Helicopter." he looks around and asks, "You did all this before I woke up?" The kitchen is spotless even that one stain Marco had been trying to get out for years is gone. Excalibur casually nods his head and makes breakfast for himself. Compared to the hard manual labor of The Valley and everything he did there, cleaning an old man's house is simple. Marco reaches across the table and holds Excalibur's hand, "I really appreciate this son." Excalibur puts his other hand on top of Marco's and they smile at each other. Marco always wanted a son, in this moment he's never been happier.

They finish breakfast, Marco goes upstairs to use the restroom. Again he's shocked that his bathroom is as clean as it is, it even smells nice. He looks at himself in the bathroom mirror, "Look at you old man" he says to himself, "The fight is almost over we have someone to pass the torch to." he lifts belly and drops it, "You're old and fat how long can you keep fighting like this." he bares his teeth at his reflection, "Hopefully there's no hell, I don't think we can be forgiven for what we've done. We're gonna pay for what we've done for a one day old man, we can only run for so long and if I'm being honest my legs ache and my joints hurt." He attempts to slick back what little hair he has, it doesn't work, he goes downstairs where Excalibur is waiting like an eager golden retriever puppy.

They go into the backyard, Marco points at the lawn and says, "Mow this and I'll show you my helicopter." Excalibur runs off to find the lawn mower, Marco shouts, "It's in the shed son!" Excalibur gives him a thumbs up and retrieves the lawn mower. He attempts to start it, Marco is sitting in an old rocking chair he yells, "It needs gas there should be a can in the shed somewhere!" Excalibur looks through the shed, behind, under, and on top of things, he finds the gas can next to a rusted motorcycle that's missing a front wheel. He fills the lawnmower and cuts the grass with deadly efficiency. He doesn't have to double back on any spots, he cuts the lawn perfectly before Marco can finish his sweet tea.

Excalibur whips the sweat from his brow and asks, "How did I do?" He's smiling and panting. He stands proud of his work.

Marco slowly stands up and looks at the backyard. He pats Excalibur on the shoulder, "Well I'll be damned that's one hell of a job. Alright, I guess I can show ya my chopper now pull the tarp off there." Excalibur eagerly yanks the tarp off, the tarps falls into a pile, in front of him is a war machine.

Excalibur touches the handle then pulls his hand away he asks, "Can I?"

Marco nods his head and says, "Go for it." Excalibur swings the door open and climbs inside. The inside of the helicopter isn't dusty, it's almost spotless, the chairs in the cockpit look like they've been newly reupholstered. Marco climbs inside, "Ya know, these are the same ones we used in the war. I got this one for cheap at a collectors' auction, ya should've seen the thing when I first bought it, all covered in rust, black widows calling the passenger seat home, rats living in the seats, and it only had one blade. I paid more for delivery than I paid the auctioneer." He sits in the pilot's seat and grips the handles, "She's almost ready to fly now," he says this with grandiosity while looking out the windshield. He pats Excalibur on the back, "Not yet though I still need to do a few more repairs and give it a cool paint job!" he hardly laughs as he stands up, "I need to head into town to run some errands wanna come?"

Excalibur stands up, follows Marco out of the helicopter, and into the house. Marco puts a pair of slippers on and tosses the keys to Excalibur, "Your driving" Marco says.

Excalibur fumbles to catch the keys, "Oh I would" he stammers, "I've just never learned how," he laughs slightly embarrassed.

Standing up, now with slippers on his feet, Marco yells in a jolly sort of way, "Well you're gonna today boy! Luckily for you I drive an automatic so you won't have to worry about shifting. They don't make too many manuals do they?" Marco throws open the front door.

Following him out, Excalibur chuckles, "I wouldn't know I've never been car shopping."

Marco gets in the passenger seat, "It was a rhetorical question son. Don't be shy, get behind that wheel, it won't bite." Excalibur opens the door and sits in the driver's seat. He rests his hands on his legs. Marco is stretched out and relaxed; he patiently waits for him to put the key in the ignition. Eventually Excalibur realizes what he needs to do, he puts the key in the ignition and turns it, nothing happens. Without looking Marco says, "You need to put your foot on the brake for it to start, that's the one on the left." Excalibur presses the brake, turns the key, the car starts. "Right it's in park son, you want to put it in reverse so we can back out of the driveway. Take it slow" He puts it in reverse and slowly pulls out of the driveway, "Alright we're way out here in the country so there shouldn't be any cars coming but you always wanna check," Excalibur looks there aren't any cars coming.

Marco says, "You're doing great son, now keep your foot on the brake and put it in drive." Excalibur does this, "Now take your foot off the brake" he does, "Ah would you look at that now we're rollin' alright ease on the gas don't slam it," he does, the car accelerates. "Alright now we're in the left lane you want to get into the right lane, flip up that lever on the left side of the wheel. Then turn the wheel just slightly until we're in the right lane." he does and there on the way down the road. There's silence in the car as Excalibur gets a feel for driving. Marco rolls his window down to enjoy the fresh air, the orange trees, and fallen leaves that dance across the asphalt make for a beautiful scenic drive.

A truck approaches from behind, Marco taps Excalibur on the shoulder, "Hey boy let this guy pass you're going ten below the speed limit pull onto the shoulder," Excalibur is hunched over the wheel and is gripping the steering with both hands. He pulls onto the shoulder and lets the red F-150 speed past, on the back of the truck are a few bumper stickers. One of them reads, God hates fags, another reads, This machine kills liberals. On the back of the truck are also a couple of flag stickers, a confederate flag sticker, and a thin blue line sticker. Marco points and says, "I fucking hate people like that."

Excalibur gets back on the road, he asks, "People like what?"

Sitting up straight and holding the grab handle he yells, "Dumb redneck pieces of shit like that! White supremacists, homophobic motherfuckers who impregnant their sisters then sit in a bar with all their shit kicking buddies and talk about how same-sex marriage is a sin or some bullshit!"

Excalibur wasn't expecting this, he builds some courage and says, "Hey Marco, can I tell you something?"

Marco turns to look at him and says, "Sure, go ahead." he gives Excalibur a kind smile.

Excalibur says with his voice shaking, "I'm trans," his fingers are tapping on the steering wheel.

Marco laughs, "Yea no shit dude, I mean you pretty much told me that anyway on the train when you told me about how your parents wanted a girl and all. I was listening to you and I was thinking, 'Why isn't he just saying he's trans' But I get it you were explaining like I was an old man. Do you need anything, for that I mean, they sell testosterone over the counter at the CVS in town."

Excalibur wipes tears from his eyes, he can't stop smiling, he reaches over to hold Marco's hand while keeping one hand on the wheel, "Thanks old man."

Marco is smiling too, he laughs, "No problem son." Excalibur gets the hang of driving on the way to town. He's no race car driver, but he's comfortable. Marco slides the Dolly Parton album, *Jolene*, into the CD player. Marco's arm is hanging out the window, he's watching the rolling countryside pass them by, the grass is a bright verdant green, the white fluffy clouds are rising from the horizon into the blue sky, and the oak trees that sprinkle the hill-sides are shedding their orange leaves. They drive over a riving crossing, there's a park ranger making sure no one is fishing the trout swimming upstream.

They reach town halfway through the album and park at the grocery store; they let the song *Highlight of My Life* finish before they get out. Marco pulls a cart out of the cart return and gives it to Excalibur; he pushes it through the parking lot and into the store. Everyone is staring at Excalibur. It feels like their eyes are piercing his skin, their hatred is palpable. Mothers pulls their kids away from Excalibur as they pass, he's not looking at them but Marco is glaring back. When the bigots of this small town meet Marco's eyes, they look away. Marco pats Excalibur on the back and gives him a hug from the side.

They do this because they respect Marco as Veteran more than they hate Excalibur for being trans. The people of RattleSnake Point hate everyone who is different or unique, they have a perfect plastic world they've constructed around themselves. They don't acknowledge rattlesnake season, because it would ruin their fantasy of a quiet suburban life. When realtors sell houses in the town, they don't tell prospective homeowners about the wildlife. When a bobcat stole a kid that was playing outside his parents watched the animal carry the kid away by his neck then told everyone he ran away, they did this so the evaluation of their home wouldn't go down. The wildlife in RattleSnake Point is an open secret, nobody discusses it. They kill snakes if they see them, but say nothing. If they try to, they're treated like they're crazy, they might even get a visit from the sheriff.

Excalibur is treated the same way as a dangerous threat that must not be acknowledged but quietly taken care of. They can look, stare, and talk about it behind closed doors, but to speak about who he is as a person publicly is taboo. Everyone in RattleSnake Point has these secrets, most of the town is wealthy and all their kids are coked up alcoholics. After cheating on their wives and snorting crushed pills off other men's butt holes on Saturday, they go to church. Excalibur isn't like them, he's honest about who he is and isn't afraid to be himself.

Marco and Excalibur go inside the store, they shop for produce, and other basic things that they need. Marco asks, "You want anything son?" when Marco calls him son five people turn their heads to look, Marco looks at them, they look away.

Excalibur thinks about it for several seconds, "I've never had soda."

Marco looks shocked, "You've never-" he doesn't finish his sentence. He speeds walks to the soft drink section and puts almost every variety in the cart's underside. "Alright BOY, well today you're gonna have soda!" He emphasizes boy daring the other people in the store to look then laughs, "How come you never had a soda?"

Excalibur sighs, "Well… this is gonna sound dumb my biological mom thought that sugar was sinful and would corrupt my mind. Sorry, that's embarrassing for me to say."

Marco laughs, "What a crazy bitch!" people turn to look at Marco, "What I served this country, risked my life for you people and I can't say bitch for fuck's sake!" they look away in shame. Marco winks at Excalibur. At checkout, Marco uses his veterans discount and gets twenty percent off his entire purchase. The cashier refuses to look at Excalibur, but he shakes Marco's hand and thanks him for his service.

If Marco wasn't with Excalibur, it's likely they would attempt to beat him. That's what they do to people who don't conform in RattleSnake Point. Last month two high school boys were beaten so badly they had to be hospitalized, the guys who attacked them weren't charged with a crime because their dads are wealthy, they're also popular and on the football team.

After the grocery store, they go to CVS to buy testosterone for Excalibur. While looking at the different medications on offer, comparing their dosage, and how many to take a few guys from the football team approach them. One of them says, "Who's that for you little faggot?" He's speaking to Excalibur.

Marco is crouched down looking at testosterone on the lower shelves, he slowly stands up and looks up at the oversized drug addicted teenager with neglectful parents. He asks, "I'm sorry what was that?" the teenager starts to repeat himself but Marco punches him in the nuts. He swings, Marco dodges, punches him in the face, then rolls under his legs. Another one of the football players tries to punch Excalibur who dodges it to the left then punches him in the left side of his jaw, which breaks it from the part that attaches it to the rest of his thick skull.

The one who hasn't thrown a punch yet runs away, the one with the broken jaw tries to say something but losing control of his facial muscle makes this hard. The one who called Excalibur a faggot turns around to fight Marco, but while he wasn't looking Marco jumped on the shelf above them, he drops down and hits the fucker in the back of his head. Blood is pouring from the mouth of the one with the broken jaw, he tries to throw punches but he's too woozy; he collapses from blood loss.

Excalibur and Marco beat the absolute shit out of the last one. He's begging them to stop but they won't, when they're finished with him he's a quivering mess on the CVS floor, he's pissing, shitting, and covered in blood. Some of the blood is his, but it's mostly the blood from his friend lying next to him.

When they finish Marco reaches down, he picks up a bottle of testosterone and casually asks, "How's this one?" he squints at the bottle to read it, "Take one tablet, two hundred milligrams, every week… then it goes on to list side effects," he kicks the football player they beat the shit out of, "Is this the one you take faggot?" he groans and nods his head. They step over the mess they made and go to checkout.

The cashier looks at why they're buying, then looks up at them, she looks disgusted, "Is that all?" Marco takes a pack of gum and places it on the counter. She rings it up, Marco pays for it and they leave.

Excalibur asks, "Are you sure they won't get us in trouble?"

Marco laughs, "Who the guys we beat up?" he says the next sentence with a sarcastic tone, "Oh yea sure they're gonna run home to their daddies and tell them they got beat up by a fat old man and a boy half their size!" Excalibur laughs. Marco asks,

"You wanna drive?" Excalibur shakes his head. They get in the car and start the drive home, Marco asks, "Where did you say you ran away from again?" Excalibur tells him, "Oh there, there was a couple that come from here a lesbian couple that ran away after the entire town fucked with em and went there. Last we heard they drove off a cliff and died."

Excalibur turns from looking out the window to look at Marco, "They tried to kidnap me I'm the reason they crashed!"

Marco scratches his chin, "Yea I figured when you were telling me about your life that sounded familiar but I didn't want to jump to conclusions. It makes sense that they would kidnap you though, they were constantly denied adoption for bullshit reasons. The real reason was them being a same-sex couple, but state funded adoption agencies aren't allowed to deny for that reason no more. Must have lost it, poor ladies I couldn't imagine what they went through." Marco looks like he's about to cry, he turns the stereo up, they drive the rest of the way home in contemplative silence.

Excalibur makes a potato soup for them, when they sit down Marco asks, "So killing?"

Excalibur says, "What about it?" then eats a mouthful of soup.

"When you killed another human for the first time, how was it?"

"Oh, horrible It felt like all the energy was drained from my body. I had seen people die before then, you know about them, but to actually end a life myself. It's not like the movies man, in movies it's this over the top spectacle blood shoots out everywhere and it's dramatic. When it happens for real though it's quick and over, a human is dead and that's all there is to it."

"You've killed other people since the first, right?"

"Yes, a lot of people." Excalibur says this quietly, he asks, "Does it get easier?"

Marco gets up to get a beer from the fridge, he sits back down and takes a swig from it, "Yea son it gets easier and that's the worst part. When I look in the mirror, I see this dark aura surrounding me, I can hear them, they're haunting me. I don't think I'll ever be forgiven for what I've done." He whips tears from his eyes, "Hold on to that as long as you can, the regret and sorrow, it keeps you human son. When you lose that you won't know what you're capable of and you'll hurt the ones you love." He reaches across the table and holds Excalibur's hand.

Interlude 2: What We Found At The End of Everything

You step outside to smoke, something you haven't done in a long time. You look up to see dark clouds gathering. Across from you in the balcony of another apartment complex you see an old woman. She's smoking too, she doesn't see you, she's staring off into space, her face is gray and weathered. She looks up at the gathering clouds and shivers. You finish your cigarette, snuff out the butt with your heel, then go back inside, and make a cup of tea. You sit down on your recliner and turn on the TV they're interviewing a madman who says there's a future. You laugh at him.

You put on your boots and walk out the door. You stand on the edge of your street and wait for them to come. Sleeks black robots pour from the streets and select the combatants. Those they don't select are given rations and sent back inside. You are chosen; you don't resist; you know better than that. You hear screaming from down the street as you're gently captured and put in a transportation pod. There's a nice comfy chair for you to sit on, you fall asleep on your way to Mega Death Dome 3000: sponsored by Disney.

You wake up being ejected from the transportation pod onto the hard, cold white floors of the arena. Lights shine on you, in the bleachers of the Mega Death Dome 3000: sponsored by Disney you can see the silhouettes of the crowd. Aliens from every corner of the nine galaxies, they cheer and make bets on your life. You don't care, a rack of weapons rises from the floor next to you, you choose your instrument of death, a katana. You've seen the show before and always planned on picking the katana if you were chosen.

On the other side of the arena you see your opponent, it's the old woman you saw this morning. She has a cut across her stomach; you assume this is because she tried to fight back. She's holding a barbed wire covered bat. The countdown starts, you feel something for the first time in a long time, excitement.

When the Murder Horn: sponsored by Gatorade sounds you run at her, she runs away. The crowd laughs and cheers.

One of them throws a rock into the arena using their chucking tentacle, this is a common snack on the alien's planet. The old woman trips over one of them, without hesitation you stab her in the neck with your katana. She reaches up and grabs your arm, her face livens up and she smiles at you. You lick her blood from the sword, the crowd roars.

The people running the show love how lively and blood hungry you are; they drop another opponent into the arena. For dramatic effect they open the ceiling to let the rain in, this causes the old woman's blood to spread. The cool rain soaks your face, you take a deep calm sigh, letting the downpour wash over you.

Your next opponent is revealed, it's a baby. The announcer comes onto the loudspeaker and says this, "Friends and enemies you've seen the killer take the life of an old woman but can they kill a baby!" This is run through a universal translator. Your hands sweat, your arms shake. The little baby is wearing a pink dress and rolling around cutely on the floor, she's playing with the old woman's blood.

You approach her; she looks up at you and giggles; you raise your sword, then bring it down on her. Her head falls off her body, you pick it up and throw it into the crowd. The announcer is ecstatic, "Friends and enemies I give you The Slasher, a true villain and killer, hide your younglings from this one!" he laughs, you're numb. He continues, "Let's see how The Slasher does against The Crusher!"

The Crusher is a fan favorite. He's a massive hulking monster of man. In last week's program he killed a class of elementary school kids with his bare hands, they screamed and ran from him. You saw this; you watched it while you drank a beer-like-product.

The Crusher roars then runs at you, his stomps create dents in the arena floor. You stab him through the chest; he grabs your head and crushes it between his hands; the crowd is going wild. The parents of the kids he killed are dropped in, they're all armed with knives, they stab The Crusher until he's dead. You fall to ground your ears are bleeding and you have a skull fracture. The parents are escorted out and you're taken to the medic. The medic bot is a sleek white robot with a red cross on its chest.

While you're being carried out you hear the announcer say, "What a fight! Thanks to our friends at Benchmade Knife Company for the tools used by those revenge seekers! Coming up, two friendly dogs with knives taped to their heads!" His chipper voice has become a comfort to you. You consider getting knives from Benchmade Knife Company. Intense invasive surgery is done on you to get you back in fighting condition. You will kill for the rest of your brief life, one day you will die by the hands of another opponent and they will be the next champion. The cycle will repeat.

Part 3: Bambi's Delight

Two years pass and Marco finishes repairing his Vietnam era attack helicopter, he names her Bambi's Delight and gives her a shark paint job. He also fits guns to the war machine, during this time Excalibur's voice deepens significantly and he grows stubble, he's growing into quite the handsome man.

Marco is the pilot for the debut flight of Bambi's Delight, he pulls up on the flight stick and screams with joy. Excalibur is manning the helicopter's gun. They're both wearing headsets so they can communicate during the flight. They're robbing a bank that a bunch of crooked cops are using to funnel drug money through, they have a thorough plan they've talked through. Marco showed Excalibur floor plans on a whiteboard, they looked at security camera footage, and know when the guard takes his break.

Before they land Marco asks, "You ready kid!"

Excalibur yells, "Ready Dad!"

Marco lands with the front of the helicopter facing away from the bank, this gets the attention of everyone inside; they have to move fast. Thankfully, it's a slow business day. The only people inside the bank are one customer, and a couple tellers, the manager is at his daughter's baseball game. Marco wears a Richard Nixon mask, Excalibur wears a George W. Bush mask.

Marco kicks down the bank door and yells, "Alright, this is a fucking robbery!" During his speech Excalibur is controlling the tellers, they both have AR-15s, Marco has his gun aimed at the single customer. Excalibur yells, "Don't fucking move old man! Don't be a fucking hero, that goes for you behind the counter too, the man with his gun aimed on you is as crazy as they come!" Excalibur uses zip ties to bind the tellers' arms to their legs. He apologies to them while he does this.

The customer says, "You'll never get away with this you-" Marco hits him in the back of the head and kicks him in the stomach.

Excalibur says, "Alright, I need to get into the vault where's the fucking manager!"

One of the tellers he has bounded cries, "He's at his daughter's baseball game, but the code is reset every day he wrote it down for us before he left!"

"Where the fucking is it, you fucking fucks!"

"Right there on that sticky note!" The teller is looking at the computer monitor closest to Excalibur, he yanks it and runs to the vault. He puts the code in and the alarm goes off. It's on a timer, the police are on their way. Excalibur and Marco don't need to talk about what's happening, they talked about this contingency. Excalibur is carrying two duffle bags he puts as much money as he can fit into one then tosses it out for Marco who throws it over his shoulder. He fills the other and they run out of the bank together. The customer attempts to shoot them in the back with a gun he was concealing, he misses, Marco and Excalibur riddle him with bullets.

They get in Bambi's Delight and start to make their escape as the police are arriving. Excalibur jumps in the gunner's seat, he shoots them as they get out of their patrol cars, one them yells into their radio, "Holy shit dispatch you wouldn't believe this there's a-" he's turned into a holey man before he can finish his sentence. Bambi's Delight takes flight and they escape the scene of the crime.

Police and FBI are swarming Marco's house, going through everything. They're analyzing the planning board that was left in the kitchen, Marco knows they're fucked he says, "Shit dude we're fucked we need to go South!" The cops and FBI agents surrounding his house hear and see the helicopter. Which isn't surprising, it's not the least bit subtle. They attempt to chase Bambi's Delight, but she's faster than they are. Excalibur falls asleep in the gunner's seat during the flight, there's another chase with border patrol as they cross the border, but that ends quickly. So quickly Marco didn't even know he was being chased.

They reach the army base in Mexico late into the night. Again this was planned for, they learned about and studied this base; they planned to fly here if things got bad. It's a small base mostly auxiliary in nature, the soldiers on the base get bored, right now they're all drunk, fat, and happy. Marco yells, "Hey kid, we're almost there get yourself ready!" he stretches and chugs a Red Bull.

Upon hearing Bambi's Delight hovering above their base, all the soldier's stumble outside. Excalibur shoots them in their bodies and faces with a massive gun that makes enormous holes, this turns the soldiers into dead people. There aren't that many on the base, maybe a dozen or so. They sweep the camp and take out the rest who are hiding, one of them is the captain who was just fucking a prostitute before they came to the base; the captain and her prostitute are both killed. With the camp clear, Marco refuels Bambi's Delight.

They sleep on the base in cots, Marco wakes up with a backache but it's rare that he doesn't. They steal the captain's pink Cadillac and go to a bar to get breakfast. The bar has swinging saloon doors, and it's on the outskirts of town. All the windows are broken and boarded up, a tumbleweed rolls by the bar. Excalibur pushes the swinging doors open, he walks in, Marco follows behind. Everyone is staring at them as they come in.

The tension in the bar is thicker than mashed potatoes covered in molasses, they sit at a table, a waitress comes around and asks them what they want in Spanish. Excalibur doesn't speak any Spanish, Marco attempts to use what little Spanish he knows to ask for two glasses of orange juice, eggs, and toast. He fails miserably. Thankfully for them, imperialism spread English to every corner of the world. The waitress asks, "English?" Marco nods his head and orders again in English.

The bartender turns on the TV, there's an emergency report that wanted men are on the loose and in Mexico. Their faces on the small television mounted above the bar. Footage of them robbing the bank and escaping via helicopter is being shown, them committing murder is being shown; the blood is censored for sensitive viewers.

Excalibur and Marco try to stand up to escape, but they are sat back down by the patrons. Before they know what's happening, they're surrounded by dozens of dangerous looking men. One of them has a scar across his eye, another has the thousand mile stare of a killer. One who has a toothpick in his mouth and a tattoo of a gun says in English, "Where do you think you guys are going huh?" his accent is a mix of French and Mexican, there's a pause the entire bar is quiet before he says, "We need to welcome new friends and hear how you guys did it!" he slaps Marco on the back and shouts, "Let's get you guys beers and tacos!" Everyone in the bar cheers.

The French man who bought them beers and tacos sits down with them and they talk for a while. He explains where they are, "You're in a bar without a name. This is the home away from assassins around the world, you wouldn't know it, but there's people in this bar that are responsible for the deaths of dictators, world leaders, and drug lords." he chugs a beer. "See that guy over there," he points to a man in a barret, "He's the leader of a rebel faction looking to violently overthrow the Mexican government." He gestures in a circular motion, "There's also various assorted criminals you know: bank robbers, drug dealers, burglars, murderers, pimps, and war criminals. You'll both fit in famously here!" He gets up and sits back down with his friends.

Marcos leans in and whispers, "I bet we could put a crew together here!" Excalibur smiles and nods. "Alright son, look for anyone interesting, I don't like boring people!" Excalibur looks around the bar for anyone who stands out, there's very few people like that most of them are large men with tattoos. He spots a lady standing next to the jukebox, covering her left eye is an eye patch, she's wearing a motorcycle jacket.

Excalibur walks up to her and asks, "You looking for a crew?"

She looks him up and down, "Maybe I am," she extends her hand to be shaken, "Felicity."

"Excalibur, wanna see my dad, he needs to know if you're interesting enough to join our crew."

Felicity laughs, "Sure kid" she sits down with Excalibur and Marco.

Marco says, "Alright lady let's hear you story"

She combs her short black hair to one side with a pocket comb, "Well, first I'm no lady guys! I'm as bad as they come. Where do you want me to start?"

"The beginning," Marco says, "You know like your story how did you end up here Felicity?"

"Strap in boys," she chuckles, "Alright well I've always been a rotten apple, I didn't do well at school, you know fighting girls who talked shit and smoking behind the school. Always in detention. This one time in middle school the teacher stepped out class and while he was gone, I took a shit on his desk. Nobody ratted me out; they knew better than that. The deuce I dropped was on top of some tests we just turned in so we all got A's."

She chuckles and then looks away to compose herself, "One day," tears are welling in Felicity's eyes, "My old man was drunk when he came back from a friend's place, I was in my room reading a book and listening to a *Paramore* CD. I heard him come in. He was yelling at my brother because he made a sandwich and didn't wash his plate. I heard my dad stomp up the stairs and into my brother's room next to mine," Felicity is staring into her drink, "Then I heard him beating my brother, he was crying and screaming and begging our dad to stop. So I ran down the stairs and I took a knife out of the drawer, ran back up the stairs, then I jumped on him and stabbed the big drunk fucker in the back of the neck. He screamed and blood gushed out of him, I stabbed him again and again. I went into a furry."

Felicity orders another drink, "Alright so our old man laid there dead, my brother kicks him then hits me, he hugged me and cried. I cleaned my brother up and tended to his wounds. When the sun went down that night we buried him in the backyard. Eventually what I did was found, my brother was sent to live with our grandparents and I escaped.

"I was homeless for a while, ran from place to place. I made money by tricking creepy old men into thinking I was a prostitute then killing them in their most vulnerable state and taking their money. Well, one day I killed some gang member apparently he was a big deal, his gang made me a deal. Do a hit on a rival captain of some biker gang or they make me a sex slave. So I do the hit and that's how I got into this line of work."

Marco asks, "How did you do it?"

Felicity is in the middle of sipping her drink, she finishes, "The hit on the rival captain?" Marco nods his head. Felicity takes another swig of her drink, "Well the dude was a biker yea and didn't wear a helmet so I studied the route he took from his house to their clubhouse. I put road spikes and waited, the dude ran over them going like eighty miles, crashed and died."

Marco smiles, "Damn that's brutal well I'd say you're in the crew," he looks to Excalibur, "What do you think son?"

Excalibur raises a drink, "Welcome to the crew, Felicity!" They cheer and drink to new friendship.

It wasn't long until a man with a lollipop in his mouth walked up to the three who were casually chatting. The man is muscular and stout, he's bald and has a short beard. On his left arm is a scorpion tattoo, on his left arm is a tattoo of a chocolate bar halfway out of its wrapper. He's wearing a blue floral shirt, denim jeans, and leather snake skin shoes. The sweet toothed stranger pulls up a chair and sits with the three. He puts his hand out and introduces himself, "Azucar," he says, he has a thick Mexican accent. Excalibur, Marco, and Felicity introduce themselves.

Felicity looks him up and down and says, "How long have you been listening?"

Azucar laughs and says, "Long enough to know that I want to join you guys. I gotta tell you my story right, why I'm in this bar and all that?"

Marco says, "You guessed it brother."

Azucar orders himself a bottle of screwball whiskey, "Alright well I didn't have a choice, My father was a member of the cartel. When I was really little he tried to hide it from me but he couldn't hide it forever. One day these guys came for him. They shot up our house, my dad killed them. There I was seven years old in footie pajamas, my dad was covered in blood surrounded by bodies, my old man said, 'Go to bed buddy I'll be up soon to say goodnight'.

"An hour later he comes up and talks to me. He tells me that those men deserved to die, that it was them or us. He kisses me on the forehead, hugs me, and says goodnight. When he hugged me, he left a bloody handprint on my shoulder.

"He stopped hiding after that, he told me where he was going and what he was doing. His honesty about his work was too much I wish he had spared gory details, now I can hear that stuff without blinking but I was only a kid then. I didn't get into the work until my twenties. When I worked for the cartel I did all sorts of things, running drugs and guns, assassinations, robbing our rivals."

Excalibur asks, "And Azucar is that your real name?"

Azucar sarcastically says, "Is Excalibur yours friend? Of course it's my real name, it's what people call me and what I want to be called!" he gives Excalibur a threatening look, "Only kidding friend!" he says with a laugh. "I picked up the name when

I was running the candy shop we used to smuggle cocaine out of. That place might still be around. I'm not sure I can't exactly show my face in Guadalajara.

"Right, right I forget to mention my friends! I'm wanted dead by the cartel," Azcaur laughs and takes a swig from his bottle of whiskey, then takes a bar of chocolate out of his shirt pocket and takes a bite. "You probably want to know why, so these bastards asked me to set some bombs off and frame a rival. The idea was to get the police to crack down on them. So they wanted me to blow up civilians, one of the targets was an orphanage, another was a church, and the other target was a hospital. I wouldn't do it, I don't kill fucking civilians!" Azucar is clenching his bottle of whiskey, he's staring at the table. "That's when I left, now I'm a freelancer."

Excalibur raises a drink to him, "You have my vote!" he says with a cheer. Felicity joins him, then Marco. All three of them have their glasses raised to Azucar. They toast to new friendship, drink bar songs for hours, and annoy the other patrons.

Eventually they're kicked out the bar, they move the party to a construction site that was abandoned. "We need a name for us" Azucar says sloppily, "Our thing you know the four of us I was thinking Mictlan."

Felicity laughs, "What's that?" her cheeks are red, and she's swaying.

Azucar burps, "The Aztec city of the dead, scary biker girl!" he chuckles.

Felicity playfully pokes him, "Who are you calling scary biker girl!" she has a bottle in her left hand that she's taking large swigs from. Excalibur has already passed out into Marco's lap. Felicity yells, "What's up with him… can't hold his booze?"

While stroking his hair Marco who's hardly drunk says, "The boy is only eighteen, and he's never drunk before I'm surprised he lasted as long as he did with you two" he chuckles and looks into the twinkling sky.

Felicity and Azucar have a drinking contest, there is no clear winner because they pass out onto each other. Marco isn't watching them because he's lying down staring up at the stars. He looks at Excalibur then looks up at the pitch black sky dotted with pinpricks of light and a big glowing moon; he pats the boy then falls asleep.

They wake up to the smell of morning dew carried by a soft breeze; they wander back to the bar and get their vehicles. Excalibur, Marco, and Azucar get in the pink Cadillac. Felicity follows behind on your motorcycle. They're headed to the nearest town to get breakfast. The diner is in a small town, so the Mictlan arriving causes a huge scene. They walk into the dinner and find a booth, everyone moves out their way as they walk through. Felicity takes off her leather jacket and hangs it behind her when they sit down.

Their waitress is terrified, she gives them extra attention. Being the only one that can speak Spanish Azucar orders from the rest of the Mictlan. Marco orders sausage, bacon, eggs, a quesadilla, and a coffee. Excalibur orders two cups of coffee and two breakfast burritos. Felicity orders scrambled eggs, avocado toast, and a glass of orange juice. Azucar orders three stacks of blueberry pancakes, two stacks of chocolate chip pancakes, a milkshake, an order of bacon, and asks for a new bottle of syrup.

Waiting for their food Azucar says, "Hey Excalibur my friend! Did we tell you the name for our crew yet?" In the middle of sipping his first coffee Excalibur shakes his head, "Mictlan!" says Azucar triumphantly, "It's the Aztec city of the dead, get it because we're," Azucar whispers, "Killers."

"Nice man, I like it," Excalibur says.

"See I knew he would like it didn't I tell you I would like it," He's looking at Felicity she's smiling politely.

Felicity calls the waitress over, "I'm sorry do you have tea?" Azucar translates this interaction.

Panicked, the waitress says in Spanish, "Yes ma'am we have tea. What kind of tea would you like?" sweat is dripping from her forehead and her hands are shaking.

After thinking about it for a moment, she asks, "Green tea?"

"Yes green tea, absolutely right away ma'am" the waitress runs off nearly bumping into an old man. She comes back with a green tea as quickly as one will brew, she moves so fast she nearly spills it on herself.

Their food arrives and everyone eats everything they ordered. Azucar mixes the bacon he ordered with his pancakes, then drenches them in syrup. When the bill arrives Marco pays for it in cash, he hands the waitress two hundred dollars. She stands there for a few moments of stunned silence, thanks them, then runs off. The Mictlan leaves, returning to the military base to plan their first job as a crew.

Felicity finds a whiteboard in a supply closet, on it she writes, "Heist ideas" Mictlan is sitting around throwing out ideas while Felicity writes them down. Excalibur yells out, "White House!"

Felicity says, "Too big, but I like the spirit!" they throw around ideas for a few hours by the end they have fifty-seven ideas. They spend another hour and a half narrowing it down to five. A bank job on a cartel owned bank, a train heist, a sperm bank heist, intercepting an arms deal, and stealing luxury cars.

The first one they cross off the list is the sperm bank heist. They decide that it's a good idea, that it would be fun, but they can't figure out how to make money from it. The next one they cross off the list is stealing luxury cars because they can't find a luxury car dealership within a hundred miles of their base. The third one they cross off the list is the train robbery because they need a quick score and waiting for a train carrying valuables would take too long. The last one they cross off is intercepting an arms deal, the danger of it would be too high for a crew's first score and it wouldn't be worth the money, they'd also have to find someone to fence the weapons, a connection they don't have yet, a connection they would need for goods that hot.

The cartel bank job is decided because it would be lucrative and low risk because there's only one guard in the bank. Azucar knows his way around the bank, he also knows that they're too sloppy and is betting that the codes are the same from his time with them. The only reason that nobody has hit the bank before is because you'd have to be crazy to piss the cartel off that badly. It's an open secret that it's their bank.

The Mictlan pulls up to the bank in an ice cream just before closing the same day, there's a large pink ice cream cone painted on the side of the truck. The ice cream is glistening, it's so well painted it looks real. Someone without depth perception might attempt to lick it. All three of them step out of the back of the van wearing different animal masks and carrying pump action shotguns. Marco is wearing an eagle mask, Excalibur a lion mask, Felicity a jaguar mask, and Azucar a panda mask.

"This is a goddamn fucking robbery" Excalibur yells, "Stay calm, stay cool, and you'll make it out of this alive!" Azucar repeats this in Spanish. Felicity knocks out the armed guard who's standing near the entrance. Marco restrains the tellers, then goes to the vault with Azucar. Azucar puts in the code for the vault, 1810, he swings open the massive vault door, which makes a low creaking sound as it opens. Inside the vault are towering stacks of cash, jewels, and gold.

"Alright friend, only take the ones with blue markings on them that's the cartel's shit!" Azucar shouts this jovially. While filling their bags with cartel loot he says, "We're regular Robin Hoods huh?"

Marco pats him on the back and says, "You got that right! Let's get the fuck out of here!" They leave the vault and make their way back into the lobby. Just as the Mictlan are about to leave, a cartel lieutenant comes into the bank to make a withdrawal. Seeing the band of robbers, he takes out his sidearm and points it at Felicity.

"Don't fucking move do you daft bastards know who you're robbing?" he yells this as loud as he can. This happens as Marco and Azucar are coming back into the lobby. Marco, Excalibur, and Felicity all have their guns aimed at the lieutenant. Azucar has the barrel of his gun pressed against the back of the man's head.

"We know exactly who we're robbing," Azucar says with a bitter anger.

"Azucar?" he says with a tinge of sadness. He lowers his gun and turns around to face the man with a gun against his head.

"I'm sorry Benedicto, I wish it didn't have to be like this," Azucar is holding back tears, he lifts his mask so the man can look him in the eyes. "You were always good to me, when I fucked up you got my back and saved my ass more times than I can remember. I wish-"

"No, it's okay brother… I'm glad it was you, this life was gonna get me sooner or later," they hug, Azucar puts the barrel of his shotgun in Benedicto's mouth, tears are pouring from his eyes, down his cheeks and wetting the gun. Azucar screams then pulls the trigger, Benedicto lays dead in a pool of his own blood and viscera. Azucar stares at him, at what he's done for several seconds, he pulls the mask back over his face then leaves the bank, the rest of Mictlan follow him out. They get in the van and leave. A minute after they leave, a single police car and twelve SUVs filled with cartel members pull up to the bank. There's yelling, mourning, and holes punched in walls.

The drive back to the base is deafeningly silent.

"Hey man, if you want to-" Excalibur says

Azucar cuts him off, "It's fine I just need to think" Another word isn't said for the rest of the drive. They quietly watch the world go by.

They let a couple weeks pass before they start spending the money they made, the first thing they buy is a nice beach house near the Gulf of California. After getting themselves settled in and turning it into a fortress, they buy guns, a shit ton of guns, and enough ammunition to take over a small nation. If there were any small countries left to conquer.

The Mictlan enjoy the luxury of their new beach house for a few days before deciding they need to make more money. Marco meets a man in a shady bar, the bar can only be reached on foot by walking through a slim path of cleared forestry. Marco learned about this bar from a blind man who only spoke in Harry Potter quotes. The shady man in the secret bar is the best fence in Mexico.

This man's name is Lord Loss, and he doesn't just work with anyone. Marco tells them of the things The Mictlan have done, Lord Loss nods knowingly. "I've heard of you" he says, "We wouldn't be speaking if I hadn't," he tells Marco about a boat in excruciating detail and tells him what he would like the Mictlan to steal for him. This will be a test, merely a taste of the fortune Lord Loss can bring them.

The sun sets over the Gulf of California; The Mictlan are speeding toward the USS Churchill, the boat skips over the pitch black water, in the water the moon is being reflected, salty sea air is on the wind, it's freezing cold. Their motorboat crashes against the mighty vessel, The Churchill doesn't notice this, it's like a nat hitting flying into an elephant. In sync they throw their grappling hooks at the railing, Marco doesn't join them because he can't climb a grappling hook in his age, and they need someone to stay with the boat.

The crew is dressed in all black, they're wearing black gloves and black balaclavas. The loot they're after is being held in a storage closet, a man on the inside who owes Lord Loss a favor painted an X at the bottom left corner of the door frame. Most of the navy men are sleeping, this is why they went in at night, the only people wandering around the boat are a skeleton crew. A few of them are stabbed and thrown overboard by the Mictlan, Felicity strangles one man. Excalibur looks away while she does this it's excruciating, the man turns blue while she squeezes the breath out of him. All the bodies they throw overboard hit the water with a thud, it sounds like their bodies are breaking just before they sink into the black.

They're on the Churchill for fifteen minutes before they find the right supply closet. "What are we looking for anyway boys?" Felicity says after going through a box of canned corn.

"Uh, the guy says we'll know it when we see it," Excalibur says.

"Which guy," Felicity asks while cutting open another box.

"Lord Loss, the guy we're doing this job for," Excalibur says this with the same tone one would use if they were asked what color the sky is.

Felicity laughs, "Sorry I wasn't really paying attention when Marco was going over the plan I've just been following your lead. When we pulled up to the boat I was thinking, cool a boat job at night this will be fun," Excalibur smiles at her and chuckles.

While they were talking Azucar was speeding through boxes, he finds one with a brown burlap sack inside, he pulls out a couple fist sized diamonds and sarcastically asks, "You think that this is what we're after." He holds the sack up so they can see how big and bulging it is. Azucar throws the sack over his shoulder, they exit the supply closest, make their way to Marco is waiting, climb down the grappling hook ropes, and speed away. When they're a mile from The Churchill the alarm sounds, spotlights are shone on the water and search boats are sent out.

Marco pushes on the throttle, everyone holds onto whatever they can hold on to, Excalibur throws up over the side, Felicity throws up from seeing him throw up, Azucar eats a handful of gummy bears.

Fifteen minutes pass, they crash into the beach, there's a man waiting for them in front of a black Mercedes with tinted windows. Azucar hands the man the sack full of diamonds, he opens the trunk, puts them in, then takes out two briefcases, he hands one to Felicity and the other to Azucar because they happen to be the closest people to him. The man opens the driver's door and says, "Lord Loss will be in touch" then gets in and drives away. The amount of money they were given would make the pope blush.

Marco says, "We did well didn't we," the other members of Mictlan chuckle because this is such an understatement it's an absurdity. Azucar maintains his composure while receiving the money in the dining room, but laughs like a madman when he gets into his room. Felicity throws it under her bed, takes her pants off, then goes to sleep. Excalibur humbly takes the money, not realizing the amount he has in his possession is a fortune, he never thought he'd have as much money as he currently has, he couldn't imagine it. Not that long ago when he didn't think he would survive his teens.

Felicity knows exactly what she wants to buy as soon as they open, she heads to the Kawasaki dealership to buy a new bike. She finds a yellow and black one she likes, "Ma'am please get off the bike" the salesman says, "You can't afford it."

She points, "How much, I want this"

"That bike is twenty thousand dollars-"

"I'll take it," she opens her backpack and hands the man twenty-five thousand dollars, "Give me the keys, keep this off the books, and I won't let your boss you almost lost a sale because you're a sexist asshole." the salesman is seething with rage.

Through gritted teeth he says, "One moment ma'am" he comes back and tosses her the keys. She catches them, puts them in the ignition, turns the key, then speeds off. She flips the salesman off as she leaves. The bike is a tiny portion of her new fortune. When she comes back, the other members of Mictlan walk outside to check out the new motorcycle in the driveway.

"You like it kid", Felicity asks Excalibur.

He looks it over then says, "Yea it's nice I… uh… dig it!" he smiles and laughs at himself.

"You got a ride?"

"Oh, uh no I don't, should I get one?"

"'Should I get one?' the kid says, of course you should man, maybe not a motorcycle but you need a pair of wheels especially at your age. Good looking, wealthy, funny, and sweet! You'll have to beat them off you!"

He blushes, he's never thought about himself in that way before, he hasn't had time to think about who's attracted. "I like those bug ones what are they called?"

"Oh, a VW that would be cool and the weather around here is nice you get a convertible. A fancy date around your arm maybe."

He laughs, "Stop" his cheeks are bright red.

"I'm just fuckin' with you kid, but if you ever need a wing lady let me know." She walks inside, lets herself fall onto the couch, then turns on the tv.

Azucars invites Excalibur to go candy shopping with him and offers to cover him. They go to a local place that lets you serve yourself, where you pay by the pound. Azucars fills multiple bags with candy, "So my friend, how do you like it, this life I mean?"

"It's good we've only done a couple jobs and I've got more money than I know what to do with. You're all really nice too, we feel like a family. Marco feels like a dad, you and Felicity feel like cool older siblings." He fills two bags with hard caramel candies.

"Put those on the counter," the owner is standing behind the counter, there are dollars in his eyes. He calls his husband and tells him to cancel any plans he has for the night because they're going out for dinner at a nice restaurant. Azucar says to Excalibur, "I like it too, this is the best crew I've been in, very determined and focused. You're all super nice. That thing about you living monkeys was bullshit yea?" Azucar drops the arm full of bagged candy on the counter and politely nods to the owner.

"Nah, that's all true," he says with a chuckle as he fills another bag with chili covered mango gummies.

"Even the thing about you being able to jump like ten feet in the air or something ridiculous like that."

"It might be higher than that I haven't measured. It's probably higher." The owner is taking the bags of candy from them as they're filling them.

"I gotta see that when we get out of here friend."

"You got it man. Thanks for bringing me by the way I'm not sure if I thanked you yet."

"You did, thanks for coming. This is more fun and I look less like a crazy person when someone is with me. Have you ever had these?" He's holding a lollipop with a scorpion inside of it. Excalibur shakes his head. "They're good, you'll like them!" He fills a bag with them. They each fill several bags with all sorts of different sweets then go to the register to check out. The mountain of candy that's pilled is so tall that they can't see the owner. He tells them the total then asks how they'll be paying, Azucar tells him they'll pay in cash, they do. The owner helps them load the candy into the car.

The next day a woman who works for Lord Loss comes to the house. He arrives while Excalibur and Marco are playing catch on the beach, Azucar and Felicity are in the living room eating sour gummy worms. They're watching *Death Proof*. The woman knocks on the door, she's wearing a red hat, a red dress, red lipstick, red flats, and her nails are painted red. Azucar answers the door, she curtsies, "Yea what's up Red Lady?" he says.

"Who the fuck is at the door?" Felicity yells.

"Some lady dressed all in red!" Azucar yells back.

The lady in red says, "If you would allow me to introduce myself. I work for Lord Loss, he has another job for you if you're interested. May I come in?" Azucar tosses a sour gummy worm in his mouth and show's her in. She sits on the couch next to Felicity, she puts her hands in her lap. Azucar steps out the back door, goes down to the beach where Excalibur and Marco are playing ball. He tells them about the lady in red and who she works for. They follow Azucar back inside, making sure to wipe their feet so they don't track sand in.

They sit around the Red Lady. "What's the job?" Marco asks.

"Yes" she says, she removes a folded slip of paper from her red bra. She unfolds it, "It's a train" all four members of the Mictlan lean forward simultaneously with interest. "There's an armoured car you'll rob next week, it's black with red trim, there's a symbol on both sides of the car and the top of the car, it's a snake eating its own tail. The car is full of gold, when you get inside push this button," The lady in red hands them a button in a glass case, "You push that button and a truck will come just toss the gold in and you'll be paid on the spot. Any questions?" Excalibur raises his hand. "Yes sweetheart."

"How will we escape?"

"Oh, yes," she flips the paper over, "When the exchange is made you'll jump off the train on the side of the track facing toward the road. You'll wait for a baby blue limousine to pick you up. The man driving the limousine will ask, 'Have you heard the news?' one of you must answer, 'Gabriel is sounding his trumpet. The end is here' if you do not say this you will have to walk home or get a cab I do not advise this. The journey home would be hot, long, and difficult even without the tremendous amount of cash you'll be carrying. Any questions?" Nobody indicates in any way that they have questions. "Excellent," she says with a smile, "Will you accept the job?" They do and shake hands with the Red Lady. She burns the paper with the instructions, then hands them another piece of paper with the time and location of the train. She bows politely to them, then leaves.

Felicity and Azucar go back to watching *Death Proof*. Marco says to Excalibur, "Hey son do you have a car yet?"

"No, I've been meaning to get to it but-"

Cutting him off, Marco says, "Ah no time like the present son bring some money we'll go get you one now." Excalibur goes to his room, takes his money out of the hiding spot under his floor board, he takes out two hundred thousand dollars.

"Is this enough?" he asks while holding out the money.

Marco laughs, "It should be unless you're looking to buy a supercar." Excalibur shakes his head no. "Alright then my boy let's go." They walk out the house and get into the pink Cadillac. Marco takes the money from Excalibur, puts it in the glove box, then turns the ignition and puts the top down. "What kind of car you want, kid?" Marco asks as they're driving down the road.

"I think a Beetle would be cool," he replies with a smile.

Marco Declares, "Alright, a beetle it is. They don't make that car anymore, so we won't be able to get one at a dealership. There's some used car places around here and they won't ask questions if you're paying with cash." The fresh sea air rolls over them on the drive, the twinkling bay smiles at Excalibur as they pass, and the sunshine is soaking them.

They pull into the parking lot when the midday moon is hanging in the sky, waiting for the sun to sink into the bay. Excalibur finds a yellow Beetle he likes, the car is the color of a sunflower. The salesman is on them, he's a vulture circling a dying man that's crawling across the hot desert floor. The man asks, "She's a beauty."

Excalibur is already annoyed with this man, "Yea, that's why I'm looking at the car."

Not getting the hint, the salesman says, "Did you see the fully automatic drop top?"

Excalibur glares at him, "Yes I have eyes, can I get in to look at the inside."

"Of course sir," says the salesman in a disgustingly saccharine voice, "I'll be right back."

He comes back a few minutes later with the keys. Excalibur takes them, not listening to a word he has to say. He gets in the car, then turns it on, he looks at the mileage, he steps out the car, he points at it and asks, "How much?"

"Ten thousand, sir," says the rotten, slimy salesman, "Are you gonna buy it without a test drive?"

Excalibur scoffs, "Do I need to? Is it a piece of shit?"

"Ah no sir, that's just uncommon sir. It's ten thousand."

"Twelve cash." Without waiting for an answer, he goes to the pink Cadillac and takes twelve thousand out of the glove box. He hands it to the salesman. "Are we good?" The salesman drops the phony smile, he looks at the cash in his hand, counts it, then looks up at Excalibur. He nods once, Excalibur gets back in the still running car, puts the top down and drives back to the beach house.

Later that night while eating dinner as a family Azucar says to Excalibur, "Hey man, I saw the car outside it's nice. Those are real fun."

Excalibur replies, "Oh yea, I had a great time driving next to the shore on the way back. It only cost me twelve thousand."

Felicity laughs, "Only? Kid, at your age I literally killed for that kind of money, you never learned the value of a dollar?"

Marco jumps to his defense, "Hey give my boy a break. He lived with monkeys for years and is the hardest working person I know!"

Felicity playfully punches Excalibur on the arm, "Ah chill old man, I'm just giving the kid a hard time." The rest of the dinner is uneventful; they talk shit, joke around, tell stories, and drink wine. They all sleep soundly that night. The rest of the week leading up to the train heist is serene and beautiful. It's a week of leisure and familial love.

Excalibur sees an old man sitting on the beach a short distance from the section of beach behind their house. He looks like he wants to be left alone, he's wearing a blue shirt with donuts on it, his feet are buried in the hot sand. He's staring at the water contemplatively. Excalibur stares at him for a long while, an usually long amount of time to stare at a complete stranger. The old man has long white flowing hair, and a long beard that reaches into the sand. The man slowly gets up, he holds his hips, stretches his arms into the air then touches his toes. He walks into the bay. Excalibur waits for him to walk back out with seaweed hanging from his beard and a fish in his hand. He doesn't, he's gone.

The day of the train heist comes, the Mictlan are sitting above a tunnel the train will drive through. The tunnel and the track leading up to it is surrounded by forestry, thick luscious forestry. An environmental group fought as hard as they could to stop the track from being built and the tunnel from being dug, but they failed. They got a few concessions; the forest remaining being one of them, and the limited amount of construction equipment used to build the track to limit the environmental impact. This was considered a victory. The thick forestry and the tunnel provided a perfect cover for the Mictlan, who are perched above, waiting. Birds are twiddling, and a deer eats a flower out of Excalibur's hand while they're waiting. Felicity takes a picture of this beauty with a Polaroid camera. The picture prints, she shakes it so it will develop, looks at it, smiles, then tucks it in her pocket.

They can hear and feel the train before they see it, Azucar picks up their bag full of guns and ammunition. They all stretch and get ready to jump onto the train. Especially Marco, because a bad fall could kill him at his age. The train gets closer, it's horrible massive gargantuan engine scares off the wild as it approaches, it shakes the earth as it scrapes along the iron. They jump onto one car as it passes under them, laying flat so they don't lose their heads where the tunnel narrows further in.

They all safely make it on top of the train, the sound inside the tunnel is deafening. After several minutes, the tunnel ends and opens into a vast expanse of green rolling hills. The Mictlan are almost at the back of the train and none of the cars behind them are black with red trim so they run across the top of the train looking for the right one.

Marco barely makes every jump the rest of the crew watch with bated breath each time he has to jump from one car to another. When they reach the right car, the rolling green hills are behind them, they're in a desert that's getting flatter as they speed through it while clinging to the top of this train. Azucar takes a rechargeable power saw out of the back and cuts a whole into the top of the car. The crew jumps in and starts bagging the gold, Felicity yells, "Oh shit wait push the button!" Excalibur takes the button out of his inside jacket pocket, flips open the glass case and pushes the button. Marco unlatches the train doors and slides them open.

A short time later a truck arrives driving alongside the train, Marco and Azucar toss the bags into the truck bed as Felicity and Excalibur bag the gold. Bagging and tossing all the gold even with combined efforts of the four of them takes half an hour.

Once all the gold is in the bed of the truck, another truck comes. There's a lady standing in the bed of this truck. She's dressed all in black, she tosses the crew six duffle bags stuffed with cash. They jump off the train, rolling down a small slope just before going into the road, Excalibur and Azucar are holding two of the duffle bags, Felicity and Marco each have one. It isn't long before a blue limousine pulls up, the driver rolls down his window and asks, "Have you heard the news?"

Excalibur confidently answers, "Gabriel is sounding his trumpet. The end is here!" the driver rolls his window back up and unlocks the rear doors, they swing open automatically. All four members of Mictlan get in, the back of the limousine is obscenely luxurious. The seats are velvet, recline, and double as massage chairs, there's nine flat screen TVs, complimentary champagne, an assortment of recreational drugs, and a tiger-skin rug on the floor. Marco sleeps most of the way back to their house. Felicity and Azucar watch *Django Unchained.* Excalibur reads *The Wonderful Wizard of Oz* and starts reading *The Marvelous Land of Oz* when they arrive at the beach house. Excalibur tries to thank the driver as they leave, but he ignores the Mictlan.

They carry their bags into the house, the blue limousine speeds off. The Mictlan gather in the living room to evenly divide the money between them. The amount of cash sitting before them is astronomical and doesn't fit on their coffee table. If they bought everything they could ever want twice, they would still have more money than they could spend. Counting this money took a long time, so they ordered Chinese food, Felicity tipped the delivery man a thousand dollars.

The vast amount of money they've been counting is in the way of their way while eating. Excalibur tosses a spring roll in his mouth, then accidentally knocks over a stack of money he was using an arm rest. Felicity uses a freshly minted bill to wipe soy ginger sauce off her fingertips. Azucar is using a stack of money as a table to eat orange chicken. Marco is sleeping because when the food was delivered he ate it as quickly as he could, then rolled over on the couch. The rest of Mictlan finish counting the money and dividing it evenly, they leave Marco's share next to him on the coffee table. Counting it all took them a long while, it's well past midnight and they've all been tired for hours, after saying goodnight to each other they fall into their beds and go to sleep almost immediately. They all own very comfortable beds, but even the hardest thinnest prison mattress would feel like the warm, tender embrace of an angel after all that counting and desperately trying to stay awake.

Having gotten a goodnight's rest, Marco wakes up before the rest of his family, he makes a cup of coffee for himself and sits on the porch. He watches the garbage man, he wouldn't tell anyone this, but he always had a secret love for garbage trucks. He thinks to himself as he watches the garbage truck, "Oh that's a Heli Rapid Rail Side Loader, nice," he takes a sip of coffee. He feels he should be embarrassed for his love of garbage trucks, he knows it's silly to care what people think of him especially at his age, "Maybe I want something to hide," he thinks, "Maybe I need a secret just for myself, something no one else knows." He takes another sip of his coffee, he looks at the brown slightly milky coffee then looks at the drops of morning dew hanging from the blades of grass. "I think I'll get breakfast," he says out loud. He leaves a note saying where's going. He lied on the note, for the fun of it, the note says he's gone to stare at the sky and daydream, he signs it with his name.

He arrives at the diner, sits at the bar next to a stranger and orders a full American breakfast. He chats up the man sitting next to him. The man is a soldier on vacation, he's stationed at Fort John Quincy Adams. Marco tells him about his time serving in Vietnam, the soldier thanks him for his service and buys him breakfast. The soldier talks openly about his work at the base, too openly. Thinking Marco is a patriot, he tells him about how they hold money for large national banks before it's transferred. Marco writes all this down in the car as soon as he leaves the diner.

He returns home and yells, "We're going to America!" The rest of the Mictlan come out of their rooms, they rub their eyes, they yawn and stretch.

Through a yawn Excalibur asks, "Why are we going back to the land of the free?"

"There's a fucking base there, grab your coats!" Marco points at Azucar and Felicity, who both came out of Azucar's room in their underwear, "And put pants on! This base is used as a transfer point for a bunch of banks."

"Bank of America?" Felicity asks as she jumps into a pair of pants.

"I don't know probably" Marco shouts, "We're taking Bambi's Delight and it's gonna be cold so bring something warm!" The Mictlan pack only what they'll need for a day trip. They throw their backpacks in the truck of the pink Cadillac, then drive to the base. Everyone but Marco falls asleep on the drive, which is quite fortunate because he's driving. They wake up when Marco's stopped for gas, Azucar gets a Red Bull.

They arrive at the empty base. The smell of rot and death is still lingering in the air, echoes of the past live here. Marco touches Bambi's Delight, he wipes the dust off of her and apologies for leaving her for so long. The rest of the crew gets in the helicopter for warmth, why the base is so cold none of them can say. A permanent fog clings to their air, doors are opening and slamming shut. Felicity tells herself that it's just the wind.

Marco finishes cleaning Bambi's Delight, they're all shivering as the helicopter rises from the ground. It feels like something is trying its hardest to keep them grounded. Marco pulls up on the stick with all his strength, eventually they rise from the earth above the wretched fog, and bask in the sun's warmth again.

They fly toward the Mexican-American border, after the escape of Marco and Excalibur there was massive investment toward anti-aircraft weapons. An ICE agent aims a massive gun that's mounted on a watchtower in the desert. He shoots baseball sized explosives at Bambi's Delight. One of these hits the helicopter. It falls toward the hard desert floor; the world slows for the Mictlan they look at each other, their hearts race, they brace for impact.

Bambi's Delight crashes. The ICE agents that were following them in jeeps speed onto the crash site. They pull the survivors out of the wreckage. Excalibur is pulled out coughing, Azucar is bruised and has a few broken bones, Felicity is mostly fine just a few scratches she's screaming and kicking as they pull her out. Marco died instantly on impact. This is a more peaceful death than he imagined for himself, he always thought he would die horribly, a few times he thought about killing himself. He got a good death, doing everything he could to save his family. Excalibur screams and cries as they pull his body from the wreckage, he's kicked to the floor by an ICE agent, his tears evaporate as they hit the hot sand. Azucar hasn't realized what happened yet, he's calling out for Marco, Felicity, and Excalibur. Felicity is starring in stunned silence at what's become of Marco, she can't believe what she's looking at. Her world has gone grey, it feels like a dream, like she's underwater.

The ICE agents are waiting for their captain so they can process the Mictlan. Excalibur's screams are deafening. They inject him with a sedative for their own convenience, there's silence, horrible silence. Azucar yells, "What's happening?"

There's a long pause while Felicity drags herself back into reality, "He's dead" she says fighting back tears, "Marco is dead!" she cries.

"No, no, he can't be fucking dead. Marco, are you sure he can't be dead? How is he dead!" Azucar screams this as he struggles to break his cuffs and get off the ground. He screams and cries the same way Excalibur did. He's also injected with a sedative so the ICE agents don't have to be bothered with his screams of mourning and agony.

Felicity is staring at Marco, she's looking at the place where his face used to be, she's clenching her teeth, and shaking with rage. She's sobbing, the tears are running down her face, off her cheek onto the ground. The captain the ICE agents were waiting for arrives, Felicity isn't paying attention to what they're saying. She watches as the captain hands a dozen agents shovels; they dump water on the ground to soften the dirt, then dig a grave to bury Marco in. When they've dug a grave just big enough to fit his body in which he's unceremoniously kicked in, then buried.

Felicity watches as they heap dirt on top of him. She watches as they take a smoke break after and talk about draft picks. The ICE agents throw Excalibur's and Azucar's unconscious bodies into the back of a black windowless van. Felicity is picked up, she's staring at the place where Marco is buried through tear-filled eyes as they force her into the van. She tries to remember where he's buried, but it's an unmarked grave in the desert.

They're taken to a government black site, an off the books place that doesn't officially exist. Their holding cells are dimly lit, the walls are painted gray; they have the potent smell of cleaning products that were used to remove human excrement. Excalibur and Azucar are still unconscious when they're placed in their holding cells, they wake up in terror not knowing where they are. Felicity is conscious for this but she has a black sack placed over her head the entire time, the sack is removed, the dim light is blinding. She instinctively tries to cover her eyes with her hand but cannot do so because they are tied behind her back with zip ties that are cutting into her wrists.

Felicity is faced against a wall with a gun pressed against the back of her skull. She's told not to move until the agents leave her cell. Her zip ties are cut, they slowly back out of the cell with guns trained on her. The thick metal door clunks shut and sophisticated locking mechanisms seal it. Felicity turns around, puts her back to the wall, lets out an exhausted sigh, then slowly sits down.

Azucar wakes up a few hours after he's brought into the cell. Startled he looks around, he looks up at the ceiling; he bangs on the metal door of his cell. He screams, then he cries, kicks the door, and punches a wall. The wall is made of solid concrete, his punch does nothing. The only sound that's made is the sound of his knuckles breaking. The camera in his cell zooms in on him.

Excalibur wakes up after Azucar, the concrete floor is cool against his face, it's almost pleasant. He rolls onto his back and stretches, looking up at the drab paneled ceiling. He looks at the door, then up to the camera which is facing him. He looks around at the concrete room and knows exactly where he is. Without getting up, he swivels himself to face the wall opposite of the door. He kicks his feet up on the wall, his body is making an L shape. He puts his hands behind his head and sighs in a bored, detached manner.

Azucar is the first one taken in for questioning. He's gagged and black bagged then taken to a room with a single lamp. He's sat in an uncomfortable wooden chair, this chair was designed by the CIA to be impossible to sit in comfortably. Azucar is strapped into this chair with his arms and legs bound to it. The black bag and gag are removed, an ICE agent in a solid black suit steps into the room, he says in a calm corporate voice, "We know what you've done if you cooperate, this will be a lot easier. I can make your life very difficult, don't make me do that." Azucar spits on his face. The agent removes a handkerchief from his front pocket, wipes the spit off his face, then places it back in his pocket. After doing this he punches Azucar in the mouth, the chair falls backwards, which causes him to hit the back of his head on the hard concrete floor.

"Now that was a warning, sir, we're going to do an honesty test. What's your name, your real name?" The agent says with an icy rage.

Azucar looks up at the agent and says, "Azucar"

"Your real name!" the agent yells.

"Azucar!" he shouts back, "What's your name, friend?"

The agent takes off his tie and undoes the top button of his shirt, "You can call me Sir Hugo Drax, you will not refer to me as Hugo or Drax."

Azucar smiles, "What's your real name?"

Sir Hugo Drax laughs as he sneers, "You're real funny" he opens a briefcase and removes a pair of pliers. He holds Azucar's mouth open, clamps his tongue, and pulls on it. Azucar screams in pain, Sir Hugo Drax stops, "Ready to talk?" he asks calmly. Azucar spits blood onto his shoes. "I'm going to leave to speak to your friends. You better hope they don't tell me what I want before you get a chance." While Azucar was being tortured, Felicity and Excalibur were prepared.

Felicity is hanging from the ceiling by her arms, the tips of her toes just barely touch the ground. Sir Hugo Drax enters the room, "Hanging in there he asks?"

"Fuck you!" she yells, "Who the fuck are you people ICE yea?"

Sir Hugo Drax runs a pocket comb through his hair, "No I don't work for ICE but they're friends of ours. Felicity Gorman, you're a very dangerous woman, do your friends know just how dangerous you are?"

"Of fucking course they know," she snarls, "Why would I lie to them?"

"To protect them, to protect yourself. Azucar seemed quite surprised by some of the things I told him about you."

"Azucar knows everything about me, we're best friends!"

"Your mother?"

"Don't you fucking bring her up!" tears are welling in her eyes.

"Did you tell him about how you murdered her, how you tied her to her bed and set the house on fire? How you listened to her scream as the flames enveloped her?"

"You motherfucker I'll fucking kill you!" she shakes violently causing her to spin and swing slightly. Sir Hugo Drax steadies her, then turns her to face him.

"You're a fucking sadist Felicity, a monster! Killing you would be a mercy, how long will it be until you kill them all, what do you call yourselves Mictlan?"

"Those people are my family I swear if you hurt-" Sir Hugo Drax steps out of the room, slamming the door as he leaves. He goes into Excalibur's torture chamber, between them is an electric field. "Ah, Excalibur, or should I say-"

"Don't if you say that name I will destroy everything, I will reduce you to ash!" Excalibur's teeth are gritted and his fists are clenched. Sir Hugo Drax says the name Excalibur was given at birth. Excalibur screams in rage, he uses sheer will and a churning anger to push his way through the electric fence. "Don't! You can't get through, you'll kill yourself" Sir Hugo Drax shrieks. Thousands of volts run through his body as he forces himself to pass the electric field, "Up the voltage, fucking stop him!" They do, this doesn't stop Excalibur he powers through, he towers over Sir Hugo Drax who's fallen to the floor, he holds his hands up in defense. Excalibur punches him, sending a bloody tooth flying.

"Is this what you've been using to torture my family, you fucker!" Excalibur holds up the briefcase. Sir Hugo Drax tries to escape the room, Excalibur grabs him by the leg causing him to fall and hit his chin. "You're trapped in her with me, you bastard!" Excalibur kneels on top of him and goes through his briefcase.

He finds a taser, he presses it against Sir Hugo Drax's neck, sending a shock through his body. He takes out a tool labeled nail remover, it's flat with a sharp tip. Excalibur digs it under his torturer's pinky nail and uses it to remove the nail. Excalibur removes all twenty of his nails this way, Sir Hugo Drax is a quivering mess after this.

Excalibur asks which rooms his friends are being kept in, Sir Hugo Drax tells him after having the spine punisher used on him. Before leaving Excalibur breaks his legs with a yellow wrench named Daisy, then forces him into the electric fence he was being kept in. "You can't just leave me here!" Sir Hugo Drax cries as Excalibur leaves him there.

Outside of the torture room are two special agents, Excalibur beats them to death with Daisy. He uses the least bloody agent's jacket to wipe Daisy clean. Outside of the advanced integration room eleven Excalibur hits the agent over the head with Daisy creating a massive crater. He swings open the door, Azucar looks up at him, "Excalibur my friend!" he smiles. Excalibur cuts him free. "Give me a second young friend, that bastard did a number on me."

"You got it man," Excalibur says, "Just stay here I'll get Felicity. Take this." He gives Azucar the dead agent's gun. The alarm is sounded, blinking red lights drop from the ceiling, and a siren blares. Excalibur runs to advanced integration room seven, outside are ten agents.

Excalibur runs at them and kills two of them before they know what's happening, "What the fuck was that!" one of them yells.

"Holy shit, Debby and Ryan are fucking dead!" scream another.

Excalibur jumps from a standing position into the ceiling panel above him. He crawls through the ceiling drops in the middle of where the agents are standing, clobbers a few of them before they react, then jumps back into the ceiling, they shoot into the ceiling but he's already dropped behind them and bludgeons a couple more. He jumps over the three remaining agents and sweeps their legs from behind. He bashes their heads in while they're on the ground, three forceful overhead swings, and they're all dead. Daisy the wrench is completely stained red.

Felicity spins herself around to look at Excalibur, "Ah dude what's up" she says then looks behind at him, at the horrible bloody mess he's created. "Holy shit dude, you are an animal!" she laughs, "Nice work cut me down!" He cuts her down, holding her up with one arm as he does so. They return to Azucar, who is laying down on the floor to realign his back.

"You would not believe how uncomfortable that chair is, friends!" Azucar shouts. He springs himself up from the ground, "Let's get the fuck out of here before the fucking cavalry gets here!" They do, and there's surprisingly little resistance to their escape. The black site is in a hidden cove off the coast of California.

A mile up the beach they find an unattended fishing boat. They climb up the side, then hide under a tarp with crab traps and nets. With a moment of quiet to think Azucar says, "He's really gone, isn't he?" Nobody else says anything. They lay quietly and wait for morning. Excalibur cries himself to sleep, Azucar and Felicity can't sleep, their minds are racing.

The hours between then and the morning are long and grueling. It feels like it will never end. Felicity is freezing and thinks she might die in that fishing boat. Before her death can come the sun rises, the captain returns to his ship, he pretends not to see the three of them hiding in the back of his boat. He goes out to the water and casts a line. An emergency alert is sent out to be on the lookout for three enemies of the state.

The captain used to be a freedom fighter, maybe if things had turned out better for him he would have helped the Mictlan. Things didn't go that way for the captain though he was ground down by the system he was tired and wanted to retire. He drinks a few glasses of whiskey to settle his nerves; he hopes that he can forgive himself for what he's about to do.

He sails his boat further out to sea, then calls Ouroboros to let them know he has the Mictlan. It isn't ten minutes before his small fishing boat is surrounded by helicopters, boats, drones, and a spider tank. All of these things are black with red trim, all have their symbol of a snake eating its own tail. Six agents rappel from a helicopter hovering above the boat, the spider tank aims its back mounted laser cannon at the tarp they're hiding under.

Three of the agents grab them, the other three are aiming guns at them that look like they're capable of destroying a tank with a single shot, which they are. The captain is given the bounty for the Mictlan, who are strapped with bomb collars and handcuffed. The spider tank opens from the front, a ramp extends out and onto the boat. The Mictlan are shoved in, A woman dressed in blue greets them, she's holding a palm sized switch, "Hello you can die or work for us. Simply pushed into the sea and blown apart. The world might even better off without you." She strokes the switch with her thumb, her nails are painted baby blue.

"Who are you people? We hit your train car, yea?" Excalibur asks with seething rage in his voice.

The blue lady removes her blue tinted sunglasses, "We are not to be known and yes you did. Insignificant things like you wouldn't have gotten our attention if you hadn't fucked with our shit. We would have left you alone to live your short life, you would have died violently fighting for what you believe in. Tell me Excalibur, did you drink from the chalice?"

Horror washes over his face, "How did you-"

"Our army toys found it, how does it work?" She says slyly, her soft hands caress his face, "Can you fix it for us sweet boy?"

"Look lady," he snarls, "I don't know how it worked the King of Monkeys made me drink out of it, there was a vine hanging above it-" The blue lady takes her hand off Excalibur's face.

"Just as I suspected they destroyed it, what a shame" she says casually, "We could have really put that to good use." She takes out a small blue bottle of hand sanitizer and uses it to clean her hands. "You all reek like fish, I assume you don't want to die so you'll work for us, right?" The Mictlan look at each other, exchange looks, and whisper about their options. They agree to work for Ouroboros, "Excellent" says the blue lady while removing their handcuffs, "Go shower, you're stinking the place up, oh and don't worry the collars are waterproof."

Interlude 3: I Wouldn't Kill A Child!

I met the most curious man the other day. I was sitting on the beach with my feet in the sand; the man perched himself like a bird on the rock above me. He said, "You know I wouldn't kill a child" I tried to look up at him but the sun was in my eyes. "I've killed a lot of things," he jumped off the rock and landed in front of me, "But a child" he leaned in, "I could never" his breath smelled of cheese and his teeth were black.

"Come with me." He said, and I followed. We walked down the beach until we reached a grove. In the grove were turtles, the man picked up a can of gasoline, poured it over the baby turtles, then threw a match. They were set aflame, the fire scorched the top of the grove, the turtles screamed, and the man laughed. When the fire died, the man turned to me and said, "See, not children."

I asked him if he killed another person, he wagged his finger and chuckled, "Ah spoilers Melissa," I grabbed his shoulder and asked how he knew my name. He smiled at me and suggested I release him.

"Do you do that a lot?" I asked.

"Kill turtles? No, there just happened to be turtles there, and I had gasoline." he said.

"But why?"

He thought about it for a few moments then said, "Well, I don't know it's something to do, I supposed. Like have you ever eaten when you're bored, even though you weren't hungry. I don't really think about it, those turtles weren't going to set themselves on fire and scream in pain. I wanted to do it, so I did. It's not complex, my girl. Would you like to join me for a drive?" I don't know why I said yes, but I did and before I had time to object or think we were sitting in his car.

I know it sounds stupid but there was something compelling about him, unnaturally so even. I knew I should have said no; I knew I should have run from him, but I couldn't. So there I was sitting in his car, "You know this is the same car that the Manson family drove when they killed Sharon Tate. A 1959 Ford Falcon." he casually said.

I should have said, "What the fuck and jumped out," but I didn't. What I said instead was, "Cool like the same model, or is it the exact same car?"

"Nah," he said, "I wish I could have gotten that car, but it's locked up forever." He turned up the radio, It was already tuned the christian talk radio station.

The man on the radio station said, "God believers, hear me! There is an evil plaguing this country, this once proud God fearing country. That evil, television, rock-and-roll music, the internet, and magazines! The only thing you should be reading listeners, the only thing! Is the bible! Anything else and you are tainting your mind with unholy lies. In fact, the only thing you should be thinking about and doing is serving the lord! If your first thought when you wake up isn't 'How can I serve god today' you are doing something wrong can I get an amen!" The stranger driving me yelled amen and hit his steering wheel.

"Is that what you do, is that what we're doing now?"

"Of course."

"The killing?"

"God put all the beautiful creatures and wonderful on this earth to die, didn't he? Isn't that our purpose, the way I see it, I'm just helping him out, saving him some leg work. Except kids I don't kill kids they're too young and I don't want to get in the way with what God has planned for them."

"Okay then, how old until you'll kill a person."

The man thought about it for a few moments, "Probably fourteen, because they've had enough as a sinful teenager and they should have learned right and wrong, so if they aren't a God believer by then they're beyond saving."

"Do you think the man on the radio would approve of your killing?"

"Pastor Holmes? He would love what I'm doing, I've always wanted to meet him but I haven't had the chance. He doesn't really do public appearances, too much jealousy, too much hate. I'm a frequent caller on his show *God Hates Us*."

We drove alongside this woman walking her dog and the man yelled, "Grab her!" So I did, he picked the little dog up by the leash then tied the leash around a tree branch. We watched and forced the woman to watch as the little white dog hung to death. The woman screamed and cried, trying desperately to break free. People walked past on the sidewalk and let all of this happen, they stared at the woman like she was in the wrong for shouting and freaking out. When the dog was dead we forced her into the trunk of the car.

The man said, "Did you see that?"

"Yea man, that was pretty fucked up."

"I know I can't believe all those people just walked past us and let that happen. Like we're clearly the bad guys, I mean killing someone's dog right in front of them and nobody does anything because it's not their problem. This is another reason I do what I do Melissa to see if somebody will care, to see if there's one decent person left out there. I'm the last honest man, I know what I am!"

We drove with that woman in the trunk for thirty minutes before we reached this cliff that overlooked the beach. We pulled the woman out and forced her near the edge of the cliff; she looked at the jagged rocks below and tried to back away. She was trembling with fear.

"You do it, push her." The man said to me, "If you do, I'll tell you my name." I put my hands against the middle of her back and shoved her as hard as I could. Her body was bludgeoned and broken on the way down. What was left on the beach was a mangled approximation of a human body, like if you gave a particularly dull alien who had never seen a human before the parts and asked them to build one.

"Francis," the man said as he stared at the corpse, "Nice to meet you." We shook hands, then he grabbed both my hands and said, "Now you're murderer aren't you, a killer? How does it feel to take a human life?"

I didn't feel anything, but that's not what I said, what I said was, "Good, powerful. Energized." I faked a smile. He smiled, a big toothy grin way too toothy. Far too many teeth. "Wanna do another?"

"Right now?" I asked.

"Yes, bigger, a bomb in a busy cafe I know about. My ex-girlfriend works there."

Again, I didn't think about what I was saying or doing. I simply agreed and got in his car, before I realized what was happening we were in his car driving to New Orleans. Francis ran over every animal on the way there.

We pulled up to the cafe at night, he pointed at it and said, "That's it we'll hit it tomorrow morning that's when the cunt is working!" At the hotel room in The French Quarter, I showered and threw myself into bed. I tried to sleep in a separate bed but when Francis thought I was sleeping in crawled in bed with me. He put his head on my stomach, his hair was greasy, it felt slimy and wet on my tank top.

In the morning I showered again then we drove to the cafe, we had a perfectly fine breakfast. When we were done Francis handed me a backpack, "Kick it under the bench when we leave" he whispered. We walked out of the cafe, I pushed the bag under the bench with my foot. It was heavy and clunked.

I got into the passenger seat of his car; it smelled like smoke and body odor; he handed me a detonator. I saw him differently; I didn't want to do it; the spell was broken, but I came too far. I took the detonator from him, my thumb quaked as it hovered above the button. I pushed it.

God was that explosion beautiful, human body parts and viscera flew out of the building. A charred arm landed on the hood of the car. It felt good for real this time.

"Would you kill a child?" he asked.

"Would you?" I asked.

"No, I wouldn't kill a child," he said, "Would you?"

I had to think about it, "No, I don't think I would."

"We'll see." He started the car, and we drove away from the scene just before the firefighters and police arrived.

Thus began one of the most violent crime sprees in American history. We killed them all, old people, the homeless, hippies, drug dealers, cops, priests, politicians, clowns, but we didn't kill a child.

We were on the run, and our time was coming to an end. Sitting in a room at the Halsey Frontier Inn, in Halsey, Nebraska. We waited, we left the room every once and while and looked at the vast expanse of land that went as far as the eye could see.

In the middle of the night Francis left when he came back I was sleeping. I was awoken by the sound of a baby crying. He flicked on the light switch; he was holding a baby swaddled in a blanket. He held the baby up like a trophy, "You wanna do this?" he asked, "Before they get us," he said this softly and with a tinge of sadness.

He put the baby on the hotel desk, the blanket she was swaddled in unraveled. The baby was screaming and naked, it also smelled like she soiled the blanket. Thunder cracked outside, and the patter of rain started against the window. "It's up to you," Francis said, leaning over my shoulder. "It has to be you that decides to do it," His long slimy tongue snaked out of his mouth and licked my face, he set a knife on the desk, then laid on the bed.

I looked at the decision before me. I thought about it for a long time, agonizing over it. I picked up the knife and felt the weight of it in my hand. I saw my reflection in the blade; it was gray and blurry, like I was hardly there. I took a deep breath, then pressed the knife against the baby's soft belly.

The crying stopped, there was no sound at all, it was perfectly silent. I looked at what I had done and I dropped the knife. There was a red glow, then Francis went into this swirling portal but just before he did he changed shape. He changed into a pitch black ghoul with long sharp nails, huge teeth in rows like a shark, and a long tongue that he threw over his shoulder.

That's the last thing that happened before the police got there and I was brought into custody. I just sat there on the bed looking at what I had done. The police kicked down the door; I didn't fight or put up a struggle; I was hollow. There was crying and screaming when they saw what I had done.

Part 4: Pink Strawberries Forever

The Mictlan shower and change into black and red Ouroboros jumpsuits. They're each forced into separate holding cells. Their cells are sterilized and clean, the smell of cleaners is overpowering.

The blue lady is sitting in her office drinking a cup of tea, she picks up her satellite Garfield phone to call her boss, "I have them, do you want them dead?"

"No, they're more valuable alive" says the man on the other end of the line.

"But sir they could destroy us all!"

"Excalibur, did he drink from the goblet?"

"Yes sir, it's exactly as we suspected, our friends in the army destroyed it with their bumbling incompetence as well."

"That's a shame, just find something to do while we figure this out."

"Yes sir." The Blue Lady hangs up the phone, she sits with her feet on the desk and stares out the window of the spider tank. Fish frantically swim out of the way of the monstrosity. A shark accidentally hits the spider tank, it's electrocuted by the tank's enemy deterrence field. The Blue Lady chuckles when this happens.

She opens her celeste blue laptop; she opens a document titled, People the CIA wants dead, Each person on the list is numbered there's two thousand and seventy-seven people on the list. She opens a random number generator; it gives her twelve thousand and sixty-one.

Goro Otsuka, thirty-one years old, Hiroshima, Japanese socialist leader.

The spider tank's private chef brings the Blue Lady a spread of cheeses and meats to snack on. She would often forget to eat and work herself to exhaustion if people didn't tend to her. She delicately picks up a piece of imported French cheese without looking away from Goro's file. She eats the slice of cheese; she picks at the spread, eating very little as she pours over every detail of Goro Otsuka's life and work as an activist.

She writes a summary of who Goro is after reading about him, then makes three copies, keeping the original for herself. She puts the briefings in envelopes, seals them with a blue rose stamp, then gives them to an assistant who slips the briefings under each of the Mictlan's cell doors. When this is done she lies in her bed fully clothed above the sheets, she lays perfectly straight on her back; she clutches a cobalt blue dagger with a coiled blade.

She does not dream.

At exactly six in the morning she wakes, she sits up in bed, looks around for danger then puts the dagger she named Ripley into the top left drawer. She starts her morning as she does every morning with one hundred pushups, one hundred sit-ups, one hundred squats, and a six point five miles run on her treadmill. She finishes, then has a cup of tea that's brought to her by the private chef. She drinks this tea in complete silence.

After finishing her tea she showers then dresses herself for the day. On this day she puts on thigh high blue socks, blue denim shorts, a blue blouse, and blue flats. She chooses to wear this to accommodate the climate of the Philippines.

The spider tank deploys its sanity cloak to hide from the people of the Philippines. The horrific and massive spider tank makes itself incomprehensible and unknowable like an eldritch horror. This technology was developed in Ouroboros' horror labs after one of the lead scientists read some HP Lovecraft.

Invisibility worked just fine before, but it fell short in a couple ways, first of all anybody could accidentally walk into whatever it is you're trying to hide. Second, they could never work out the glimmer that invisibility cloaks created, and it struggled with direct light.

The blue lady returns to her office and sits at her desk, she has the Mictlan brought to her. She asks them, "Did you read the briefing?"

Nobody answers.

They're given a painful electric shock. She asks them again, "Did you read the briefing?"

Excalibur grits his teeth and says, "Yes"

Felicity whispers to Azucar, "Did you read the thing?"

He whispers back, "No, did you?" She shakes her head.

The Blue Lady rubs her forehead, "You know I can hear you guys, right?" They stare at her. "Excalibur, please explain the assignment to them. I'll be back. I need to be away from you people right now." Excalibur explains to his friends what they'll be doing while The Blue Lady composes herself, she isn't used to having to be this patient with people who cause her annoyance. Normally she would've killed them where they stand.

She returns, they're standing around waiting for her. She asks, "Did you explain to them what we're doing?" He nods. "Okay good, here are your plane tickets you're leaving from Manila in an hour. Here put this on you're not allowed to know where the tank is parked." She hands them all thick black hoods made of canvas.

They're led out of the spider tank, spun around, walked a mile down the beach, spun around then walked a mile further then put into the back of an armoured SUV. Their hoods are removed, the SUV speeds through the city streets toward the airport.

A cop races behind them, flashes their lights and sirens. They realize who they're trying to pull over and drive onto the side of the road. The driver says nothing to the Mictlan; he has a steely focus. The stereo is blaring David Bowie, and the driving is making them all feel sick. The massive vehicle is just barely clinging to the road, all the red lights are run, and there are several near misses.

They pull into the airport fifteen minutes before the flight is supposed to take off. The driver pulls them out of the car and rushes them through the airport; he commandeers a golf cart, no one makes any attempt to stop them. They arrive at the terminal ten minutes before the flight is supposed to take off. No one stops them as the driver walks them through security and makes sure they're seated.

He watches the plane take off.

Felicity, Azucar, and Excalibur and seated in the same row. Excalibur is in the middle seat. "At least we're in first class," Felicity says as she reclines her seat.

Azucar orders a drink, and a slice of cheesecake.

Excalibur gets the attention of a stewardess, "How long is this flight?"

"Just over nine hours, sir," she smiles.

"Holy shit," he groans, he reclines his seat as far back as it will go. He tries to go to sleep but he can't, he has a million thoughts racing through his mind.

Azucar nudges Excalibur, "Hey switch sweets with me"

"You want the middle seat," Excalibur asks

"No, I wanna sit next to Felicity so we can watch a movie together. Just take the window seat man."

Excalibur asks, "Are you guys a thing?" Felicity laughs.

"No, we're just homies," Azucar says. They switch seats. Excalibur closes his eyes and tries desperately to go to sleep. He remembers Marco is gone, and that he isn't coming back. The reality hits him, he rolls over, turns toward the window, and weeps. The beauty of the sky above the clouds does nothing to soothe him, the reds and oranges in the distance mock him. The fluffy clouds reaching in all directions make him feel like he's drowning.

He rolls over to face Azucar and Felicity, "I miss him so much. It feels like he was just here, and now he's gone we're never going to see him again. Him, the monkeys, and you guys are the only family I ever had and now they're both gone. Am I cursed to destroy everyone I love?" Excalibur is sobbing, his face is red, and snot is coming out of his nose.

Azucar had been trying to push his feelings down and not think about it, but he can't bear it anymore; his heart aches and he has to let it out. He cries and tries to comfort Excalibur at the same time. Azucar being emotional only made him more Emotional they are both sobbing on each other.

Everyone else on the plane is trying to pretend it's not happening, including Felicity because she has her own methods of going through mourning. The circumstances of Marco's death and their subsequent capture have just prevented her from doing what she normally would.

Azucar and Excalibur cry themselves to sleep on the plane in each other's embrace. Felicity watches a couple movies, reads, and watches an episode of The Sopranos for the remainder of the flight.

They land at Hiroshima airport. Felicity wakes her friends up, they get off the plane and walk out of the airport. Outside of the airport there's a massive man dressed all in black, he's standing in front of a black Mercedes Benz with dark tinted windows. He looks at the Mictlan and says, "Jesus Fucking Christ, why do they dress you guys like that and what's up with these bulky collars. Come here." He steps over to the trunk, opens it, removes a briefcase, closes the trunk, and places the briefcase on top of it.

The seven foot tall man built like an oak tree rummages through the intentionally disorganized briefcase. He takes out three watches, and three black credit cards. "Here, put these on and use these to get yourself something decent to wear."

They put the watches on, which automatically adjust themselves and loosely tighten onto their wrists. They are loose enough to be comfortable, but not loose enough to take off. He removes their bulky collars, "Now don't think you can go fucking around those have enough box jellyfish venom to kill one hundred and twenty people. Our mutual friends farm the fuckers. The car is yours." He tosses the keys in their general directions, Felicity catches them then tosses the keys to Azucar.

The tall man squeezes himself into a taxi, the taxi drives off. The Mictlan look at each other, "So shopping?" Felicity says, "I can't wear this jumpsuit, it feels like I'm a prisoner."

Azucar says, "Suits make me feel the same way, like there's a noose around my neck. Like I'm an imposter wearing someone else's clothes."

"I think it looks kinda cool, just not my style" Excalibur says. They get into the car, Azucar drives, Felicity sits in the passenger seat and Excalibur lays across the back to stretch. "Why does my back hurt?"

"Probably because you and this one," Felicity points to Azucar, "Were cuddled up in an awkward position for hours." There's an awkward silence, Felicity realizes what she said was rude and insensitive, "Look I'm sorry it's just that-" she stops herself realizing that what she was about to say would have made things worse. She thinks for a moment, "So a mall yea? That way we can go off shopping on our own?"

"Yea sure," Azucar says with a tinge of annoyance, he taps the built in GPS trying to figure out how it works. "Hey kid, you know how this works?"

Without looking Excalibur says, "I lived with monkeys in a remote valley then with Marco."

"Shit, you're right my bad." Azucar says, he taps the screen having no idea what he's doing.

"Here let me see," Felicity says, clearly trying to make up for what she said, "Malls" she says out loud as she types it. "Ah, there looks like this is the nearest one" She routes to the mall.

The drive to the mall is awkward and silent until Felicity says, "Hey look, I'm sorry for what I said about you guys cuddling on the plane. I'm not handling his death well either. I just haven't had time to process everything that's been going on, and none of it feels real yet. Sorry for being an incentive, asshole."

When they get to the mall and park, they all get out and hug. Say sorry some more then reassure each other that everything is okay before going their separate ways for shopping, they plan on meeting back the car in a couple hours.

Excalibur bought himself a pair of jeans, a pair of black skate shoes, a *Misfits* shirt, and a flannel to go over it. He cuffs his jeans and accessories his flannel shirt with an assortment of pins, including an anarchy pin and a pride flag pin.

Azucar bought himself twenty-seven patterned button up t-shirt shirts, nine pairs of snake skin boots of various colors, and a baker's dozen of cargo pants. He also stopped at the mall's candy shop and bought eight pounds of sweets.

Felicity bought a black poet's shirt, a few dresses, nine pairs of jeans, five pairs of shoes, sixteen t-shirts, and thirty-two jackets. She also withdraws a large sum of money and a new purse to put it in.

They met back at the car with the things they bought, Felicity looks at Excalibur and asks, "Where's all your stuff?"

"This is what a got, cute right?"

"Yea it is, but we had free rein to go on a shopping spree."

"Oh yea, I just got what I wanted. I don't really like malls, there's too many people, they're too loud, and it's just an overall bad experience. I got this in like forty minutes, then just sat around people watching until it was time to go. Oh, I did get a coffee." He gleams at them.

Azucar and Felicity look at each other and the armfuls of things they hold then back at Excalibur who has his hands in his pockets. "You're okay with you got like you don't want to get anything else?" Azucar asks.

"Yea dude, I'm totally good." There's a pause while Excalibur remembers what he wanted to tell them, "Oh right, while I was waiting I looked into hotels. There's one pretty close to where Goro is supposed to be for the rally and they have availability."

"Alright dude!" Azucar says he pats Excalibur on the back and opens the trunk. He and Felicity toss their things in. This time Felicity drives, Azucar is in the passenger seat, and Excalibur is in the back like before. The mood on the drive to the hotel is a lot better than the mood on the drive to the mall. They drive with the windows, a fresh summer breeze that smells like flowers blows through the car, everything feels okay, peaceful like they're all meant to be where they are.

They reach the hotel; the lobby is beautifully decorated in art deco style. Their room is extravagant, three bedrooms with a main room, a balcony, and a kitchen. The hotel room is on the top floor and takes up the right side of the building.

They all get the best sleep they've ever gotten and their entire lives. In the morning they all wake perfectly and in great moods. They sit around the dining room table pretending like they aren't about to do what they came to Hiroshima to do, just for a little longer they can hang on the pleasant fantasy they've created.

Several minutes of pleasantness pass.

A knock at the door. Excalibur opens it, on the floor is a black cube with red lines running along the edges. He touches the cube; it flies into the room and lands on the dining room table where Felicity and Azucar are still trying to enjoy a quiet morning.

Excalibur chases after it and watches it with his friends. The cube spins in mid air, unfolding itself as it lands. It creaks like an old ship while it does this.

After a minute it settles on the table. The unfolded cube fabricates an arsenal of weapons, each of the weapons has one of their names carved into it. The Mictlan watch all this happen in stunned silence, Excalibur turns a chair around, sits on it backwards and rests his head on his arms.

The cube finishes fabricating the weapons and the ammunition. It finishes doing this, then floats back into the air. It spins counter clockwise, folds in on itself until it turns into a red pin prick light.

All three of their jaws are agape. They say nothing as they try to process what they've seen.

The first one to say something is Felicity who says, "What the fuck dude." Azucar shakes his head and rubs his face. None of them can find the words to express the shock they are in. What can be said, what needs to be said, they've all seen something they can't explain, completely changes their worldview and what they think is possible.

After individually coming to this same conclusion, they pick up their guns and start planning the assassination of Goro Otsuka.

Excalibur is perched in a clock tower overlooking the rally. His sniper rifle is aimed directly at Goro's head, who's delivering a speech. Felicity is hidden amongst the crowd. Azucar is the wheelman, he's in an ice-cream van a block away.

Next to Goro is a woman translating everything he says into Japanese for the few old people who refuse to learn English "Hello, good afternoon comrades." he says, "We are here today to demand a change." He pauses a moment to look at the millions of people staring back at him. "We toil for most of our lives in meaningless jobs where we don't reap the value of our labor. We're given a number and told that's our name, we're prisoners. We're told what to wear, what to say, even how to feel. How many of you have forced a smile when you wanted to cry. We do this and to what ends, just to survive barely making enough to live while our corporate overlords become richer and richer making more money in a single day then the average person makes in their life. I say no more! I say-" Before he can finish Excalibur shoots him in the head. Creating a bright red splatter on the banner behind him.

There's a moment of silence and then panic, there's screaming. People are running, trampling over each other. Azucar is speeding toward the rally to extract Felicity, who's now firing at the crowd around her because they identified her as a gunman.

Excalibur dismantles his sniper rifle and packs it, he slides down the clock tower ladders and waits for Azucar. He's driving as fast as the ice-cream van will go, he speeds around the corner and barrels through the crowd, driving directly toward Felicity. She's drenched in blood and standing on a mountain of corpses. The ground beneath them which just minutes before was a fresh green color is now stained red with viscera and littered with mangled human bodies. Faces twisted into caricatures of misery. The ground is sticky, the smell of death is putrid. The air is so thick and pulpy that it has a metallic taste.

Azucar's ice cream truck is soaked with blood as he plows through the screaming crowd. People try to push each other out of the way but the tightly packed crowd fleeing makes this impossible, a path of violence is carved through toward Felicity. By the time he reaches her, the van has so much blood on it that the paint is almost completely covered. Organs hang from the rear-view mirror, the grill, the bumpers, and are stuck in the rims of the tires.

Felicity throws herself in the van, Azucar puts it in reverse retreading where he came through, loved ones that are attempting to save their dying family are run over. He speeds around the corner and toward the clock tower, Excalibur jumps in, they go a mile down the road, park the van in an alley then burn it by putting stuffing a paper towel in the gas tank and lighting it.

They hire a taxi to take them back to their hotel room, and they also pay him a life-changing amount of money to not notice that Felicity is covered in blood. Sitting in the back of the cab sandwiched between Felicity and Azucar, Excalibur says, "Damn, I feel so bad right now about that shit. He was making some good points too."

Felicity chuckles, "Why do think they wanted him dead. He was demanding a change to the status quo that keeps them in power. Especially with that big of an audience, he's a very dangerous man to the people in charge. Japan becomes a socialist country and succeeds, then it makes the rest of the world realize that there's a better way. The people will keep their power and wealth at any cost!"

"And that's why we killed a man because he's a threat to the global power structure?" Excalibur asks.

Azucar interjects before Felicity can respond, "No, we killed that man and all those fucking innocent people because they ordered us to! It was them or us. Would you two stop fucking talking about politics I need some quiet time to think!" No one says anything for the rest of the drive. Before getting out of the taxi, they pay the driver a small fortune to pretend he didn't hear their conversation.

They go into the hotel room Azucar goes into his room, shuts off all the lights and throws the covers over himself.

Felicity's wet, blood-stained clothes have begun to smell and cling to her. She puts them into a thick plastic bag so she can dispose of them later. She lets the water wash over her; the blood saturated water flows off her body and swirls down the drain. She rings her hair out a dozen times before the thick red lightens up, after that it takes a few more rinses before she gets all the blood out. She thoroughly scrubs her entire body several times and still blood flows off her. She's in the shower for an hour and a half until she feels clean enough to get out. A thin film of blood stains the shower floor.

Excalibur is taking a nap on the couch in the main room. He has a blanket loosely draped over himself and the TV is tuned to some trashy shopping network. On the coffee table in front of the couch there's an empty cup noodle and an empty glass of tea. Felicity gently caresses his face and smiles at him, "Oh sweet boy," she says. She tucks the blanket and puts a pillow under his head.

Felicity goes to Azucar's room and gently raps on the door. He opens it; he looks awful, his eyes are red, puffy, and bloodshot, there's dried snot around his nose, and a mark on his face from the bed. He clears his mucus filled throat then says, "Hey"

"Hey man, you look like shit," She says.

He laughs, "I feel like shit. Hey look, I'm sorry for the way I snapped at you and Excalibur in the cab that wasn't cool."

"Ah, don't worry about it man. What do you want for dinner?"

"I don't know if I can eat right now, what does Excalibur want?"

"He's conked out on the couch. I was thinking sushi does that sound good?"

"I could fuck with some sushi. Just get me whatever." He says.

"Alright man, I'm gonna wake our boy up and see what he wants." Azucar closes the door.

He goes into the bathroom and washes his face. He looks at his reflection in the mirror; he doesn't recognize the person who stares back at him. He feels like he's looking at a stranger that looks vaguely familiar, but he can't place the name.

Felicity kisses Excalibur on the forehead to wake him up, "Excalibur," she says as she strokes his hand. She kisses him on the forehead again. His eyes flutter as he wakes from sleep, he looks at Felicity and smiles.

He stretches and rubs his eyes, "How long was I out?" he asks.

"Only a couple hours," Felicity responds, "Hey I'm gonna order sushi for us do you want something?"

He grabs the blanket and rolls over onto his side to face the TV, "Spicy tuna rolls and spider rolls would be good," he says then yawns, "Oh and if they have green tea one of those too please."

Felicity orders food for all three of them and it arrives thirty minutes later. Azucar pulls himself out of bed and sits with his friends to eat, he keeps a blanket wrapped around himself while he eats; he sips his sweetened green tea holding the cup with both hands.

Before they can finish eating, there's a knock at the door. Felicity says, "Fuck me, what is it now?" she pushes herself away from the table, goes over to the door and throws it open. In front of the door is a black humming pyramid, it rises from the ground, Felicity kicks her foot under it, the pyramid doesn't react it flies past her and floats over the table. Excalibur and Azucar move everything out of the way. A hatch opens on the bottom of the pyramid, dropping a few pounds of cocaine and methamphetamine. After this it drops a note which gently flutters down on top of the drug pile.

"Hello," the note reads, "Excellent work now to frame the socialist party and vilify them. You'll find that the bundles of drugs have the socialist party logo on them. Handle this as you see fit, your next assignment will follow." The note self destructs after all three of them have read it. The pyramid drops socialist party stickers and tags before flying out of the room.

They brainstorm ideas on how to frame the socialist party. Excalibur is writing ideas down on a whiteboard, they're taking swigs from energy drinks. Ideas that they've worked through and figured out wouldn't work are crossed off the list.

One idea that was crossed off the list was dressing up as clowns and handing out the drugs in balloons.

It takes an hour before they come up with a plan.

Felicity plays the dumb foreigner she takes one pound of cocaine to the police station, she go the front counter as says, "Hi I found this and it looked suspicious" she takes the cocaine out of her bag and places it on the counter. The officer's eyes widen and she makes a call. The cocaine is taken and Felicity is questioned. She says, "I found it under a park bench when I knelt down to tie my shoe. What is it?" They let her go.

When she finishes at the police station she goes to the local highschool and hands out little baggies of meth to students. The baggies have the socialist party logos tied to them on cute little tags. Some of the students smoke the meth they were given to help them study, most of them tell their parents who call the police.

Excalibur makes packages that contain cocaine and meth. They're small brown boxes tied with gorgeous red ribbons. Tied to ribbons is a note with the socialist party logo on it, the note on each package reads, From the socialist party with love, and a little heart is drawn. Excalibur rents a moped, drives out to the residential neighborhoods, then the countryside to deliver these packages. He gently places them on doorsteps and in post boxes.

Azucar for his part goes to candy shops and mixes the drugs with the confectionaries. While at these candy shops he buys several pounds of sweets.

Excalibur is the last to return to the hotel room, the sun is setting as he's driving back. Felicity and Azucar are beginning to worry. He stops to get himself mochi after returning to the moped to the rental agency. He walks in the hotel room, Felicity runs at him, hugs him tightly then demands to know where he was. He tells her, she smiles, and hugs him again. He asks what they did with their;drugs, they tell him.

After hearing what Azucar did, Excalibur puts his hands on his hips, laughs and shakes his head.

In the morning there's a knock on the door, on the other side is an electric cowboy. A mechanical man, the gears turn in his body and he walks. He raises his shiny arm to wave, it creaks as he does this, his voice is stilted, "Hello" he says, "And congratulations" His face makes the sound of scraping metal as he gives them a big toothy smile. "You have successfully," there's a brief pause, "Framed political dissonance as drug dealers." He extends both his hands to be shaken. Felicity shakes his left hand while Excalibur shakes his right, then Azucar shakes both his hands.

"I am here to," the electric cowboy announces, "Extract you from the country. Please follow me." He leaves the room, The Mictlan follow him. They take the elevator down to the garage. He leads them to a white van, painted on both sides of the van is an electric cowboy riding a mechanical bull. There's lettering designed to look like rope above the illustration that reads, Yippee Ki Yay, "Please get in or else," says the electric cowboy.

They sit in the back on top of a few crates. The electric cowboy sits in the front seat and lets out a facsimile of a laugh, "I've got you varmints right where I want you. I used deception.exe you will not be extracted until you do one last job." He tips his ten-gallon hat.

Felicity sighs, "What do we have to do."

The gears turn in the cowboy's mechanical mind to calibrate for this contingency, "You will blow up an elementary school full of children. You will find everything you need in those crates, you do not have a choice in this matter. Refusal will result in termination of your lives. You'll be deader than a possum on the side of the road cowpokes."

Inside the crates are jumpsuits, jackets with the socialist party logos printed on them, and three strange looking devices. On the side of the devices there's lettering that reads, NYMB 99, "That stands for Not Your Momma's Bomb, the ninety-nine indicates its year of creation. I do not have a mother, for I am a mechanical man. I've never felt the warm touch of a loving mother. I've never felt any touch. I'm so desperately lonely. It sure does get cold sitting on the prairie under all them stars." The electric cowboy stares off into space, a single drop of motor oil runs down his face. He lifts his duster and wipes it away. He takes a slip of paper that was tucked inside his coat, "This is where you are to place the bombs for maximum effectiveness. Make sure you get out in time or you'll be smoked out like a gopher hole."

The electric cowboy plays Hurt by Johnny Cash on repeat and sings along while they drive to school. They pull up to the front of the school, The electric cowboy says, "I'll stay here and try not to join them galloping horses in the sky while y'all are gone."

The entrance to the school faces south this is where Felicity plants her bomb. It only takes her a few minutes, when she returns to the van the electric cowboy is holding a shiny revolver with a wooden handle to his head, he sighs and holsters it when he sees Felicity. She pats him on the back and asks, "Did I interrupt something?"

Azucar and Excalibur go inside the school, Azucar plants his NYMB in the boiler room and gets out before anybody notices him. Excalibur plants his in the cafeteria while planting it under the table a kid tugs on his sleeve and asks, "Are you fixing that table cause it's wobbly?" The kid pushes down on the table to show that it's wobbly.

Excalibur is sweating, "Oh uh yea sure… hey I saw something crazy outside the school go check it out?"

The kid looks up at him with big sweet doe eyes, "What did you see?"

"Oh uh a fairy, yea but they're really hard to see so you might have to look hard."

The kid giggles, then runs outside. When the kid leaves, Excalibur finishes planting the NYMB and pulls the fire alarm, just as he pulls Azucar is reaching for one to pull. They run out of the school with the kids and their teachers. Excalibur and Azucar get into the back of the van, "You were supposed to kill them all!" The electric cowboy yells.

He pulls the van across the street, "Those kids were supposed to die, which one of you rascals pulled the fire alarm?"

"I did," says Felicity.

"Remind me not to invite you to play liar's dice cowgirl." The mechanical man's mind churns as he goes through their files and analyzes them, "I guess you folk are thicker than sagebrush huh meaning you won't be giving each other up no matter what." His neck creaks as he turns to face the school.

A few minutes later the fire department arrives, everyone is standing outside the school. The firefighters enter the school; the bombs go off sending a plume of smoke into the sky. The children are knocked off their feet and flung into the street. A few of them are thrown into the brick wall that surrounds the school. A dozen of the children are killed instantly, three teachers are killed.

What little remains of the school collapses in on itself. The survivors don't know it, but they'll have respiratory problems for the rest of their lives. The parents of the children that died are consumed with grief, some can't bear the pain and end their lives.

The Mictlan watches the destruction of the school in shock and horror. The electric cowboy drives them to an abandoned cafe next to the river. They sit in silence for the first half of the drive, Azucar cries himself to sleep. Out of boredom the cowboy turns on the radio, it crackles to life, a woman's voice pleasant and professional, "And now a terrorist attack." She says,

"After the massacre at their rally, sympathy and approval for the socialist party was at an all-time high. It is now believed that the attack was from a rival drug operation after several pounds of narcotics were found around Hiroshima. The bombing of Sunflower Elementary is shocking, but unfortunately it might become more common as experts say this might be the start of a gang war between the socialist party and an unknown organization. Stay tuned we'll keep you updated with the latest information as we receive it."

An AD starts, "Consume Percocet! Consume Percocet! Does the gnawing pain of existence make you want to die, do you want to feel nothing for a while? Consume Percocet!"

The electric cowboy clicks the radio off, "You think that dang ol' Percocet could help an old country boy like myself?" No one says anything because they're still trying to cope with what they've done. Azucar is still sleeping, Felicity and Excalibur are staring into the distance. "Now don't be down them youngins were gonna die eventually." The electric cowboy looks at them in the rear-view mirror. He's met with silence. "Right then if you're gonna be like I'm listening to my *Waylon Jennings* CD."

At the abandoned cafe next to the river, they're picked up by a black helicopter. The setting sun is glistening on the water, the smoke from Sunflower Elementary rises and grows into a looming cloud over the city. The Mictlan move like zombies as they get into the helicopter.

They sleep during the flight. In their nightmares they're haunted by faces of death, images of bombs, the end of the world, an army of electric cowboys roam a ruined world.

The helicopter lands at an airport, The Mictlan are moved from the helicopter into a van which takes them to a dirty run-down Motel 6. They're put into a room collapsing into a pile on the floor; they fall back asleep.

There's a knock on the door in the middle of the night, a pink envelope sealed with a strawberry stamp slipped under the door. None of them wake until the afternoon.

They're covered in sweat, there are marks from the carpet on their faces and arms. They have headaches and they're exhausted despite having just slept for thirteen hours. They look at each other with bleary eyes; they stand up and stretch. Their backs ache and their muscles are sore.

Excalibur notices the envelope first, he says, "Ah fuck me with this fucking bullshit what is it now?" He tries to bend over to pick up the note but he can't because his back hurts too much so he squats to grab it. He examines the light pink envelope, flips it over a few times, then touches the strawberry wax seal.

From the hot bath where Felicity is trying to soothe her muscles, she yells, "What is it?"
Excalibur yells back, "I don't know" he borrows a knife from Azucar who's laying on the floor to straighten his back. He opens the envelope. Inside is a letter, it's decorated with doodles of strawberries, hearts, and smiley faces. Excalibur reads the

letter out loud, "Hello my sweet little loves. We've been watching you for a while and it's made us sad, your prisoners of our greatest enemy. You have our sympathies.

"We have intercepted your next assignment from Ouroboros. They want you to poison a Cuban water supply to make it look like another failure of socialism. We are watching, if you'd like our help, face the railing outside your hotel room and make a heart with your hands.

"Pink Strawberries forever," Excalibur walks outside and makes a heart with his hands like the letter said to do. A paper plane flies through the heart he's making. He opens the letter, goes back inside, he says, "They responded guys.

"Excellent choice," Excalibur reads, "When you feel the plane to Cuba get way too shaky and start to fall, activate the friendship bracelets that will be delivered shortly.

"Pink Strawberries forever." There's a knock on the door, a package, inside are three bracelets. They have one of the Mictlan names on each spelled with beads, they also have strawberry beads, and are different colors. Excalibur's is black and blue, Felicity's is yellow and black, Azucar's is the colors of Neapolitan ice cream.

They put the bracelets on and try to relax for the rest of the day, but the anticipation of another knock makes this hard. They push the beds together and watch movies for the rest of the day. They fall asleep holding each other tightly like they're afraid that if they let go they'll fall to pieces.

After a hard, restless night, where all three of them woke up in terror multiple times, there's a knock on the door. Felicity wakes up and screams when she hears this, her scream of terror wakes Excalibur and Azucar up as well.

Azucar throws the door open and yells, "What the fuck do you cunts want now?"

The electric cowboy standing there says, "Howdy partners, you're gonna help us with our pest problem." He has a big toothy smile, "Afterwards perhaps you could end my painful undying existence. Every moment for me is a waking nightmare. Did you know that I experience reality in slow motion every second for you is five seconds for me? I know I seem like a happy folksy cowboy, not so, please kill me if you get the chance."

Azucar asks, "Do you want a drink buddy, you bum me out."

"I wish I could wet my whistle with you partner, but my manufacturers have made this impossible. Unfortunately I will never know solace or peace. Please come with me, your sky carriage is waiting."

Felicity yells, "We just woke up man give a few minutes to get ready."

"Initiating sarcasm.exe," the electric cowboy says, "Sure miss I love waiting around for humans who've had the luxury of sleep. That's exactly what I want to do after standing in a supply closet for hours. No rush."

Feeling bad for their mechanical steward, they try to get ready as quickly as they can. When they finish he says, "Let's hit that long dusty trail cowpokes." He leads them to the Yippie-Kay-Yay van they rode in before. When they reach the airport they drive on the tarmac, park in front of the boarding stairs and get onto the plane. It's a solid black color that absorbs almost all the light that touches it.

Halfway over the pacific ocean the plane is hit. It shakes and wavers like an injured animal. It's hit again and begins to nose dive. The Mictlan desperately try to figure out how their friendship bracelets activate. The plane falling quickly, they can feel the heat as it rapidly crashes toward the water.

Excalibur pulls on one of the strawberry beads, which expands into a safety bubble that holds him sweetly and tenderly. He yells, "It's the strawberries pull on them!" Felicity and Azucar yank their strawberries, just like Excalibur: they're wrapped in massive safety bubbles three times bigger than they are.

Thirty seconds later the plane crashes underwater and trapped inside the plane for a few moments they fear they might drown until their safety strawberries shoot them upward through the plane, the surface of the water, then twenty feet into the air. They safely fall into the water and float like buoys.

Five minute later a pink speed boat pulls them out and deactivates their safety strawberries. They collapse and fold back into their friendship bracelets. The driver of the speedboat is a young girl in her early twenties wearing a pink jumpsuit with black trimming, the patches on her shoulders are two crossed knives on a black background with a pink strawberry on top. She's also wearing Doc Martens and a friendship bracelet like the Mictlan are wearing. This is the uniform of The Pink Strawberries.

She holds out her hand and says, "Emily," all three of them shake her hand. "I already know you guys, you don't need to introduce yourselves. Alright, so they're probably already sending a signal that the plane has gone down. I need to know that you trust me!"

Excalibur asks, "What are you going to do?"

"We don't have to have time, do you trust me?" They all agree that they trust her. She cuts off the watches they were given when they landed in Hiroshima, then throws them in the ocean, all three of them are injected with box jellyfish venom contained within the watches. They're in agony, the most extreme pain they've ever felt. Azucar feels like he's having a heart attack. Felicity goes into shock. Excalibur is violently convulsing on the deck as the venom attacks his nervous system.

Emily throws open the cooler covered in cute stickers, she retrieves the antivenom. She stabs Excalibur in the arm with the first vial injecting him, the purple liquid flows into his body. Next she stabs Felicity with the thigh and injects her. Emily is moving as quickly as she can, she sticks the last one in Azucar's arm and injects him. They all recover as quickly as they fell ill,

Emily beams at them, "We dyed it purple to make it cuter." They thank her and sit down.

She gives them sparkling water and mango slices. Once she ensures that they've recovered enough, she speeds off before the Ouroboros cavalry comes.

They're several miles away when Ouroboros reach the crash site, they comb the water but all they find are the watches and a fried electric cowboy who can only say, "Please kill," and make a fist with his left hand. He's wiped and recycled into a toaster.

The blue lady is called and informed. She calmly receives the information, delicately takes a sip of her tea, then throws the cup against the wall, shattering it. She screams, "Fuck fuck incompetent assholes! I'll have that fucking robot turned into a toaster and leave burnt pieces of toast in him!"

Emily and The Mictlan reach Hello Kitty Island at night. It's an old abandoned place, the towering rides dwarf the natural land features. The Ferris wheel is the biggest thing on the island. Emily docks the boat at Keroppi's Fantastic Island Tour. She shows them to their rooms at Cinnamaroll's Sleepy Town.

In the morning they're woken by the sound of the loudspeaker announcing, "Goooooood morning sunshines get ready for another beautiful day of resisting those who would crush us like ants beneath their boots to make an extra nickel. Don't forget your stretches!"

Excalibur sits up; he was too tired last night to notice that his room is frog themed. Azucar wakes up to find that his room is parrot themed. Felicity's room is dinosaur themed. Excalibur's pillow is a frog and his bed is a lily pad, and there's a large frog habitat. Azucar's room looks like a bird sanctuary, and next to it separated by a thick sheet of glass is a room sized parrot habitat. Felicity's room looks like a scene from Jurassic Park with the thick forestry decorating it and realistic dinosaur statues.

They go about their normal morning routines, but everything they interact with does something musical or cute. The tap water comes out of the faucet their favorite color, they test it because it's concerning. Felicity even calls them to make sure it's safe. The showers play simplified versions of their favorite songs, and the toilets thank them by name after use. Azucar thought someone was hiding in his room fucking with him when this happened.

The Mictlan meet up in the courtyard in the center of the island. There's a lush flower garden surrounding a thirty foot tall *Hello Kitty* Fountain that flows with pink water. The base of the fountain and the podium *Hello Kitty* stands on are each five feet, the statue itself is twenty feet.

Excalibur yawns and drinks out of a *Chococat* mug filled with ice coffee. He asks his friends, "Did your showers play *Dolly Parton* songs this morning?"

Felicity says, "Nah, mine played a couple of Dead *Kennedys* songs and a few from *Misfits*." She takes a sip of her energy drink.

Azucar says, "*Paganini*"

Excalibur looks at him and says, "What?"

Azucar looks up at the statue and runs his hand through the pink water while saying, "That's what my shower played this morning, songs from *Niccolo Paganini*. He was one of the greatest violinists; he was so good and so fast that people thought he made a deal with the devil." He flicks the water of his hand, "I would make a deal with the devil if given the chance."

A young woman approaches. She has pink hair, and she's wearing a sunflower dress. She moves with power and dignity. "Hello I'm Julia," she says with a bow, "It's great to finally meet you all." They greet her.

Azucar asks, "So what is this, what are we doing lady?"

"Ah, right to the point I like that! You're a man of action. A real go-getter." She points at him with her beautifully painted nails. On each nail is a different symbol or piece imagery. On her index finger is a pentagram. "You're on Hello Kitty Island. You know why you've never heard of the biggest theme park on earth and why it was never open? Human rights violations and filthy capitalists! The people who built this fucking place killed the native population and buried them in a mass grave. They poured concrete over the grave," She points to the fountain, "Then built this monstrosity so their crimes would never be unearthed.

"The dumb greedy motherfuckers weren't done yet though. They had their big fancy theme park built, but staff cost money, especially if you have to house and feed them. That's why they bought six hundred thousand Uighur Muslims from the Chinese government. These poor fucking people were unpersoned and ignored by the international community, held in concentration camps, most of them had family and friends killed right in front of them. Then they're bought by some fucking company who wanted to save a fistful of dollars. They only got caught because the boats were stopped in international waters by pirates who opened the shipping containers and blew the whistle on the whole operation. In the end the company was dissolved into *Disney* who bought it cheap, no one was prosecuted, and the six hundred thousand Uighur Muslims were sent across the world as refugees." Julia takes a deep breath and sits down at the edge of the fountain.

The Mictlan sits on the fountain with her. They stare at the horizon for a few somber moments. Excalibur asks, "How could they get away with all that?"

Julia says, "Who's gonna stop them?"

He looks at her with determined eyes, "We will!" His voice shakes and he looks like he's about to cry.

She hugs him tightly, "You're goddamn right we are! Alright, you guys down to burn a CIA poppy field in Michigan?"

Felicity sarcastically says, "Of course the feds have that."

"Oh yea," Julia says, "They sell more drugs than every other criminal organization on Earth combined. You guys in?"

"Hell yea, let's corn hole these fuckers!" Felicity shouts.

"I'm in these assholes have been messing with us for too long," Azucar says.

Excalibur is staring into the middle distance, "They took everything from me. They slaughtered my family, burned our home down, then they killed Marco. I'll do anything to get back at them. Anything! If I had to kill a baby in their crib I would. I would drop a fucking nuke if I had the chance!"

Julia looks horrified, she laughs uncomfortably, "Alright man, I don't think that infanticide or nukes will be necessary. I'm gonna tag along with you guys. I've been on this island for too long." She takes out a *Hello Kitty flip* phone and makes a call.

She leads them to the airport; they get in a pink plane that has flowers, hearts, and satanic imagery painted on it. The flight to Michigan takes twelve hours, they watch movies, play Mario Kart and Animal Crossing with Julia and talk about their feelings.

"Excalibur," Julia says to him about halfway through their flight, "Are you okay. I've been watching you since you left the valley and you aren't the same."

"I'm angry. I feel hopeless. Like there's this black swirling void in my chest and when I die, it will pour out and flood the entire world. I've killed so many people most of them didn't deserve it, they shouldn't have died. I won't be forgiven for what I've done in the end, will I?"

She looks at him solemnly for a few seconds, "You can't let what Ouroboros or their friends win. If you turn into a hate machine that destroys everything they win. Kindness is more radical than hate." Azucar and Felicity have joined them now.

Felicity says, "You're our brother you know that right, that we're family?" He nods, she hugs him. He feels like he's about to cry, he can feel the emotion welling up in chest making its way to his throat. But he doesn't, he swallows the pain and hugs Azucar then Julia.

They land at an abandoned airport on the outskirts of Detroit. Packs of hungry wild dogs roam the long concrete expanse, they eat gophers and rats; they drink from dirty rain puddles. The gray clouds of the twilight sky hang heavy as they howl, which echoes across the runway and into the dilapidated hangars.

They step out of the plane, Julia looks at the pack of wild dogs run by she says, "First the runway was a field, a beautiful meadow where wildflowers grew. Then it was a neighborhood, where people raised families, where kids played, where memories were made. Then the city got big, people said it was going to be the next New York, the Paris of the west. So they tore the neighborhood apart and built a massive airport on top of it. Planes flew in and out of all day.

"Then manufacturing jobs were shipped out of the country to places where they could charge their employees a few cents an hour, the people who actually made the companies what they are were left in the cold to starve and die. Then the CIA came and sold the desperate people drugs because they wanted to feel just okay for a bit. Nobody wanted to come to Detroit anymore because the media said it was a dangerous place, infested with drugs and gangs. So the airport was shut down."

She looks around, "I was never here back then that was decades ago. But the echoes of the past still ring through the shattered windows of this place." All four of them are looking around, grass and wildflowers grow from the cracks and potholes in the runway.

"It's getting late," Julia says with a yawn, "Do you want to burn this poppy field tonight or wait until tomorrow?"

"Let's do it right now. Let's corn hole these fuckers!" Excalibur yells.

"Alright man," Julia says, "Is that what you guys wanna do?" She looks to Azucar and Felicity.

Felicity says, "Yea sure as long we can stop to get some Red Bull or Monster on the way I'm good."

"I'm down." Azucars says he has a calm serenity about him.

Julia makes a call on her Hello Kitty flip phone. Thirty-two minutes later, a pink van with gold rims pulls up. In the back of the van are three metal barrels. The driver is a member of the pink strawberries and she's wearing a trans pride pin.

Excalibur says, "Oh hey nice, I'm trans too."

The driver says, "Nice what are your pronouns." He tells her, "So how long have you known?" She asks.

He laughs, "Since I was like five, I think. But I didn't start transitioning until my teens. How about you?"

"I was like ten," she says, "My mom noticed, so they took me to a specialist, did a shit ton of tests, then started me on hormone blockers. I started taking estrogen when I was fifteen. How were parents about it when you came out?"

"They called the people that take you away in the night to a conversion camp, so I ran away and lived with monkeys."

"Oh yea, I read that in your file," she laughs.

"You know it's funny, the monkeys were actually more accepting than my parents." They both laugh.

The driver says, "My name's Christie by the way."

They listen to *Taylor Swift's* album *1989* on their way to the poppy field. Excalibur, Christie, and Julia know all the words, they sing along the entire time. When they stop for energy drinks and snacks, Azucar and Felicity go into the store together to get away from their young friend's singing. The gas station attendant has cold dead eyes, he's sick, he looks like he's dying. He's an old man. He should be in bed watching tv not standing in some brightly lit gas station in the middle of nowhere at two in the morning.

Felicity and Azucar enter the store and the man looks at them with contempt. Felicity grabs four energy drinks, holding two in each hand. Azucar picks out some chips, he hopes that having mouth fulls of potato-like products will stop the three of them from singing for a little when they get back on the road. The low hum of the fluorescent lights is a constant annoyance to the elder gas station attendant. The bright lights and that hum give him headaches that he can't take medicine for because it will conflict with the numerous medications he's on.

Sometimes he wonders what would happen if he stopped taking the medication, the dying doesn't scare him, it's the pain. How long would he be lying there, his heart convulsing, spit and drool coming out of his mouth. He also worried about the medical bills if he's unsuccessful, if it doesn't kill him he'll be hospitalized. He stares at Azucar deciding between lime and barbecue flavored chips and thinks about killing himself. He notices the gun Azucar is carrying, a dangerous-looking man to be sure.

They approach the register, the gas station attendant touches the box cutter under the counter, Felicity puts the energy drinks on the counter. The attendant lunges at them with the knife, Azucar goes to put the chips on the counter, the knife slices through them spilling barbecue flavored chips on the floor. The old man stares at them, anticipating his own murder. The box cutter is shaking in his hand, the blue veins that run up his arm pulse.

"Shit, dude are you alright?" Azucar asks, "Here let me help" he goes behind the counter, pulls him off the counter, and helps the old man get back on his feet. Azucar sits him down and gives him water.

The gas station attendant says, "I thought you would kill me," the words creak from his mouth.

Azucar laughs, "Why would I kill an old man who had a muscle spasm?" The attendant's eyes widen, he looks away from Azucar. Felicity is cleaning the chips off the floor.

The old man looks at her and smiles, he looks down at his hands, he holds his face in his hands and sobs, "This is the nicest anyone has been in so long. You don't know what this means to me." Azucar pats him on the back. The attendant grabs Azucar and holds him. Felicity smiles at them, then gets a new bag of chips.

They finish hugging after several minutes, "Let me finish ringing you up. I'm sure you have things to do." he says.

Felicity stares at him for a while then asks, "Could you retire right now if I gave you two hundred thousand dollars?"

He laughs, "Yes I suppose I could, wouldn't that be nice but I'm su-" Before he can finish Felicity opens her purse and hands him the money.

"Here," she says, "You shouldn't have to do this shit at your age."

"You can't be serious." he says looking at the stacks of money on the counter.

She says, "I'm dead serious and I have more money than I could ever spend. Please, just take it and quit this job man." he smiles at her.

When they get back to the van, they watch him for a few seconds. He picks up the money and counts it; he checks to make sure it's real. Then he screams, a joyful scream of victory. He takes his phone out and calls his boss, telling him he quits. He throws his uniform on the ground, stuffs the money in his pockets and walks out of the store to his old beaten *Camry*. He drives off, pumping his fist the whole time.

Felicity explains what happened to Julia, Excalibur, and Christie. They nod politely but are uninterested because they wanted to get back to listening to *Taylor Swift* songs. As soon as she finishes, Christie slowly turns up the volume knob, and they erupt into singing.

Azucar is less bothered and annoyed by this than before. He found the experience with the attendant humbling; it gave him perspective. He sits back, exhales and relaxes. Seeing Excalibur happy and spending time with people closer to him in age is nice. They're telling jokes to each other and talking about things that are completely foreigner to Felicity and Azucar.

Felicity puts her head on Azucar's shoulder, he puts her arm around her. He turns to face her; she looks up at him; she leans in for a kiss; he leans in; they kiss. Neither of them can help but notice how soft each other's lips are, they hold each other tenderly and kindly. Their hearts are racing and their cheeks are flushed. They can't stop smiling.

The three in the front are oblivious to this happening behind them as they belt the lyrics from *Taylor Swift's* song *How You Get The Girl*.

Felicity smiles at them, then kisses Azucar again. She sweetly holds his face, they hold each other for the rest of the trip to the poppy fields.

They reach the poppy fields, Azucar and Felicity quickly move apart, not wishing to make whatever they are now public. They don't know what they are yet and don't want to have to explain that to Excalibur.

The poppy field is glowing under the full moon and their smell is being carried by a swift breeze. They shut the van off and get out. The field isn't silent, there's the sound of the wind moving through the poppies, owls are hooting, crickets are chirping. Excalibur, Azucar, and Felicity each unload a barrel, they stab the barrels and start rolling them through the field.

"What's in these anyway," Excalibur asks.

Julia is waking with them she says, "Acetone"

"Holy shit, we aren't fucking around!" Felicity says.

Julia laughs, "No we are not they're going to see this from space!"

They finish pouring the acetone over the field, get in the van, and drive a safe distance. Julia takes out a zippo lighter with an anarchy symbol on it, she lights it and hands it to Excalibur. He throws it into the field, it almost instantly erupts in flame, a massive raging fire that reaches into the night sky. The brilliance of the fire rivals the full moon, and the millions of stars glowing behind it.

They stand and watch the fire. Then they sit on top of the van, staring deeply into it for a long time. Too long because the deafening sound of the raging fire muffled the circling helicopters. Black with red trimming, a snake eating its own tail on the sides of the flying metal monsters.

The helicopters shine their searchlights on the van. The five of them jump off the van, Christie opens a hidden hatch built into the floor, inside is a stockpile of pink rifles. Ouroboros operatives rappel from the helicopters, several of them are shot as they descend and fall to their deaths. Their screams are piercing, then suddenly stopped when their bodies hit the ground with a thud.

The rappelling operatives who aren't shot on their decent run at The Pink Strawberries and The Mictlan. They try to flank them using the sides of the van, but they're no match and are shot before they can react. The helicopters land on all sides of the van, dozens of operatives run out of the van, they're all mowed down creating piles of bodies.

A quiet, the smell of gunpowder, and fire. The raging flame is dying. The five of them load into the van. Just when they're about to drive away a woman in a blue exosuit runs at them, they fire at her; she doesn't stop and fires back using her arm mounted machine gun. Her exosuit allows her to move swiftly toward, they are her prey. As she gets closer, they see who it is, The Blue Lady. She's gritting her teeth and has a crazed look in her eye. They speed away from her; she keeps pace and deploys her arm mounted sword.

She laughs manically, and fires recklessly at the van, causing its bullet proof casing to break down. Felicity is shot in the spine, she screams in agony and lies down across the back seat. Julia opens a wall panel using her thumbprint, inside is a rocket launcher with *Hello Kitty* missiles, she pushes open the back doors while The Blue Lady's gun reloads and fires at her.

The Blue Lady slices the missile in half. Julia grabs another one, reloading her rocket launcher as quickly as she can move, her hands are sweating and her heart is racing. The Blue Lady aims at the van as her gun reloads, Julia fires and hits The Blue Lady, blowing her back and causing her to stumble. She trips and crushes the gun under her own weight.

She activates ultra turbo mode on her exosuit to catch up with the van. The extra heat from ultra turbo mode causes her to sweat and her blue eyeliner to run down her face. She catches up to the van, and jumps on top of it, she crunches the roof as she lands and starts stabbing into it. Hot bursts of steam shoot out of the exosuit as she madly stabs into it. Excalibur and Azucar fire at her, the bullets bounce off her; she laughs.

Christie slams the breaks, going from one hundred miles to zero in half a second. The Blue Lady flies off, Christie speeds up and runs her over crushing her legs and chest. This also causes one of the heat pipes on the suit to break. The Blue Lady stands up, and gives chase again, the inside of the exosuit gets so hot that her skin boils, her agony is palpable. "Eject occupant!" she shrieks.

"Access code required." the suit says.

"Fuck fuck fuck," she screams, "Seven-two-zero-one,"

"Code accepted. Ejecting occupant." She shot out of the exosuit, her boiling skin is cooled by the wind as she floats down to ground on her parachute. It's pitch black she can't see where she is or where she's landed. She tries to stand up and finds no ground beneath her feet, she blindly reaches around her and feels the bark of the tree she's stuck in.

The Pink Strawberries and Mictlan are half a mile down the road now. The van is horribly damaged and riddles with bullets, the wind whistles through. Felicity is laying across Azucar's lap unconscious, her blood has soaked the entire back seat. They pull over, Julia bandages her wounds and stops the bleeding. Azucar is crying and holding her, "We need to take her to the hospital," he pleads.

Julia consoles him, "We can't, they'll call the police. Hey Christie, where are we?" She opens GPS and shows her, "Cool," she says, "Alright, I know a place we can go nearby," she puts the address in.

Excalibur touches Felicity's cold pale face, "Please don't die on me I can't lose anybody else." His tears wash over her.

They speed to Ron's Crazy Cheap Used cars, Julia bangs on the door of the house next door, "Ron! Ron, wake up you have a critical fucking patient!"

A large hairy mountain of a man opens the door, he's wearing a dirty white robe. "Oh, hey if it isn't my favorite fucking niece," He hugs her.

"Hey Uncle Ron can't talk my friend's shot in the fucking spine." Without hesitation he runs toward the van, they pull Julia, carry her into the house, then into the basement. Ron sweeps off a table he was building a Lego set on, it breaks on the floor, they gently set her down. Ron turns all the lights on and looks at her spine.

"Is she going to be okay?" Azucar and Excalibur ask simultaneously.

Without looking away from Julia's injuries, Ron says, "I'll try my best. Go upstairs and try to get some sleep."

They try to fall asleep but they can't, they're sick with worry, they feel like they're going to throw up. They pass out from exhaustion at seven in the morning. They all wake up in the late afternoon covered in sweat. Uncle Ron is in the kitchen making soup, Felicity is asleep on the couch, her torso is wrapped in bandages. Azucar holds her hand and kisses her on the cheek. Ron comes in from the kitchen, "She'll never walk again, but she'll live," Excalibur and Azucar sob, they hold her tightly. "Easy now guys, she's been in surgery all morning." They hug her less tightly.

Christie and Julia watch all this respectfully, then follow Ron back into the kitchen. Julia is eager to help him cook and catch up. She tells him about *Hello Kitty* Island and everything she's been up to; he gleams with pride.

Azucar strokes Felicity's hair while he sits and watches TV. Excalibur is sitting by her feet thinking about how her legs don't look broken. "Hey Uncle Ron," he yells, "Her legs don't look broken!"

"She was shot in the spin son, her nerves are severed," he yells back. He whispers to Julia, "He's not the sharpest tool in the shed is he?"

"That's Excalibur dude." Julia says back.

"Fuck my bad, now I feel a dick." He stirs the pot of soup and sprinkles in a fistful of pepper. "So he's the ape boy?"

"Dude!" Julia scorns.

"That's what they were calling him on the news when those attacks were happening on that town." Ron says defensively.

"I know, but that's fucked up." Julia says. There's an awkward silence. Christie tries to help break the tension by making a joke, but she only makes it more awkward.

Her and Julia leave to get coffee.

The smell of soup wafts through the house, Felicity wakes up, she looks around. Startled she tries to stand but falls off the couch, she realizes her legs aren't working, she screams, cries, and throws things. Azucar and Excalibur lift her back onto the couch. Uncle Ron checks her to make sure she didn't hurt herself. After ensuring she's okay, he goes back to cooking.

She pulls Azucar in, "They're going to pay for this!"

"I know" he says, "We'll do everything we can."

"No, these mother fuckers took my legs. There's a secret base in Nevada, Area 99. I've only heard rumors, whispers in seedy bars from crazy eyed men who swear they knew a man, who knew a man, who saw what they had in there. If only a fraction of it is true, we can bring all of this down man! We can build a new world, a better world." She grabs Azucar's hands, "We'll be heroes!"

He kisses her, "Get you shit Excalibur we're going!"

"Wait what? Like right now?" He says as Azucar walks out of the house.

"Where are you guys going?" Uncle Ron shouts as the door closes behind them.

They walk to the bus stop and buy tickets to Nevada. The trip is long and exhausting, days turn into nights, the gorgeous American landscape turns into endless miles of strip malls, then back into pristine land, then to miles of nightmarish capitalism over and over again. Every town looks the same, they all have the same shitty fast-food places, gas stations, and superstores. Excalibur is filled with loathing and hatred.

A local tells them about the base. He's a crusty old man, the sun has fried his brain and turned him mad. He speaks in rhyme and riddle. Following his instruction, they go north.

As they march through the Nevada desert, they can feel the grim reaper's long boney fingers reach for them. There's a horse skeleton laying in the sand, in its skull a viper has made a home. The hot desert air whips them. Sweat pours from Excalibur's forehead, he takes a long drink from his canteen. The Nevada sun beats down on them, it's harsh and relentless, not even a cloud to give them a moment's refuge. The dust being kicked up in the air irritates their lungs and eyes.

They come across an old metal shack, it's rusted, it looks like it's about to collapse in on itself. Sitting in front of it are two soldiers playing pinochle. They haven't seen Excalibur and Azucar yet, their full attention is rapt in the game. After talking about it for a couple minutes, they decide to play outdoors man.

Azucar raises a friendly hand to the men and uses a southern drawl to hide his Mexican accent, "Well howdy there fellas, what're y'all doin' out this way?"

The soldiers stand up to face the two, one of them says, "I could ask you the same thing Sir!"

Excalibur going along with the southern tourist shtick says, "Shoot me and my brother here, just out enjoying the beautiful Nevada country here!"

The soldiers lower their guard, "Well you're lost Sirs… this is a testing site… a live range," He says struggling to remember what he was supposed to say to civilians.

"Sorry fellas," Azucar says, "Say we're awfully parched, you fine gentleman wouldn't have some water, would you?"

"You know what," one soldier says, "Why don't we get you guys a ride back to civilization." He takes off his radio and starts to make a call.

Azucar yells, "Mazapan!" They attack the soldiers. Azucar shoots one of them in the head, Excalibur beats the other to death crying and screaming as he does so. Azucar pulls him off the deadman. "Let's take their uniforms, I saw a thing where this guy just walked into places with a clipboard. We'll go as far as we can before shooting, remember we're just here to expose what they're doing here man!"

The uniforms fit poorly, and they're covered in blood.

"No way they're going to buy this dude." Excalibur says.

"Not with that attitude they won't, just be confident, man!" Azucar says.

They go inside the shack, it's shining, and the polished metal shows their reflections. They step inside the glass elevator that takes up half the room. Inside is a digital panel of buttons, Azucar presses the button that will take them to the lowest level. The elevator dings and starts its descent. The vast underground structure is filled with thousands of people working on secret projects, all separated into individual cubes. In the middle of the structure in a panopticon where the electronic guardians keep watch. One of them stares at Excalibur and Azucar as they make their descent, it scans the badges on their bloody ill-fitting uniforms. Thinking they have clearance, it ignores them. Azucar takes pictures of as much as he can on their descent.

At the negative forty-fourth level, the elevator stops. The lights turn on and reveal a massive oversized hallway. It doesn't look like it was made with humans in mind, at the end of the corridor is a pair of sliding metal doors bigger than a house. One of the soldier's standing guard in front of this door peers down the hallway, the distance between him and the two Mictlan is vast he can only see that they're in uniform. As they get closer he orders them to stop, Excalibur kills them all before Azucar has a chance to talk. Azucar takes a picture of the massive doors.

When looking up at the doors from the ground, they can't see the top. There's an eye reader to open the doors, Excalibur finds the guy wearing the most medals and scans his eye. The ground shakes, the metal doors separate, a burst of cool air escapes the room.

A single light is shining in the room onto a briefcase in the middle of a circular platform. There's a walkway leading to the platform, just big enough for one person. Looking over the railing, neither of them can see the bottom. Cold air is flowing up from the endless void.

The briefcase is warm, Excalibur opens it. Inside is a laptop, he hits the space bar, the laptop wakes up and says in a pleasant voice, "Password?"

"Shit dude!" Excalibur yells.

"Incorrect." says the laptop.

"Uh... one-two-three-four?" Azucar says.

"Correct," says the laptop, "Please select up to three targets for nuclear annihilation."

"Holy fuck! We can't do this man!" Azucar says.

"Invalid selection." says the laptop.

Excalibur thinks for a few moments, he's shaking and feels like he's going to be sick, "The White House" the laptop confirms the selection, "The Pentagon" the laptop confirms the selection, "And New York City!" The laptop confirms the selection.

The laptop asks, "Are you sure you'd like to destroy... The White house, The Pentagon, and New York City?"

"Excalibur, listen to me man," Azucar grabs him as he stares at the laptop, "This is insane you're going to kill millions of people! You can't fucking do this, you'll destroy everything."

Excalibur stares at the laptop, Azucar holds him and cries, he begs him not to do it, "If you do this we're done! You'll lose everything! Are you fucking listening to me! Please don't do this!" Excalibur closes his eyes, he thinks about everything that's been taken from him. He remembers seeing The Valley burns, his first real family die horrible. He remembers the beach house, and how Marco was killed. He thinks about the bus ride, the miles of urbanization, the churning machine that destroys everything that doesn't fit into its hegemony.

He pushes Azucar away, "Felicity is lying on a couch right now. The strongest person I know is broken and she'll never get better, and you want me to forgive them for that, just let it go? You want me to forgive them for enslaving us, making us kill innocent people? I should show them forgiveness when they've taken my family from me twice! They created me Azucar, I'm their monster!" Excalibur is crying and shaking with rage. "Confirm nuclear annihilation of selected targets!"

Azucar pushes him on the ground, he yells, "No no no fuck fuck fuck!" Azucar takes off his friendship bracelet and throws it at Excalibur as he runs away. Azucar chases after him, just barely making it on the elevator as the doors closes. They sit as far apart as they can and refuse to look at each other.

They walk out of the shack. Vultures are picking at the naked corpses of the soldiers. They trudge through the desert for a while, not looking at each other or saying a word. Excalibur tries to say something but before he can get the first syllable out Azucar punches him, "No shut the fuck up!" he yells, "We're fucking done you can rot out here for all I care!"

Azucar leaves him covered in dust and blood.

Part 5: From My Front Porch you Can See The Sea

Five Years Pass.

Excalibur is a full grown man. He lives in a cottage that overlooks the sea, his backyard is a thick forest full of life. He has a full bushy beard that flows down his burly frame.

It's a simple life. In the morning he sits on his porch and casts a line into the water, while he waits for a fish to bite he drinks coffee from an oversized mug. He looks out to the twinkling water and takes in a breath. He finishes his coffee, takes what he caught back to his cottage and puts it in his ice chest. Then he tends to his garden, watering plants, and snipping weeds. He puts his hands into the dirt just to feel the heartbeat of the earth. He then chops the wood he'll need for the day, to cook his food and warm his hearth. This is his daily routine.

Once a week he hikes to the general store in town and trades the dream catchers he makes for things he can't acquire on his own. He buys coffee, rice, and pasta. He fears that one day the man that runs the general store will figure out who he is.

One day while foraging in the woods for berries, nuts, and mushrooms, he finds a strange well. A tangle of purple vines grows from the well, wrap around it, and the surrounding trees. Excalibur touches one of the vines, it quivers and recoils like a tentacle. He cuts the vine, deep in the well there's crying and anguished moans.

Fearing someone might be in trouble, he climbs down the vines. In the well is Julia, her hair is long pink and flowing, she's wearing a pentagram dress, and covered in bandages. The purple vines lift her off the ground and move her toward Excalibur. She moans in agony.

"Who… who's there?" She asks.

"Julia?" he says, "It's me Excalibur!"

"Ah, I was wondering why they brought me here."

"What happened to you?" He asks.

"After you dropped the bombs, me and The Pink Strawberries went to New York to help with the rescue efforts and give aid to the survivors. I felt responsible for what you did, so we went there and looked for anyone trapped in rubble. I saw kids whose parents had been turned to shadows on the sidewalk. Mothers clutching their dead babies and screaming on piles of ash.

"We went into the subways, led the people out of the shell of the ruined city. I found this mass of purple vines that moved like a rat king. It attacked me and burrowed itself into my eye sockets. The last thing I ever saw was it lunging at me.

"It took me Excalibur. It uses me. I'm a prisoner. It has this knowledge, I don't think it's from this world. The only pattern I've found is that it likes cold, wet places. Sometimes it uses my body to do good. Last week we helped these Russian refugees escape a gulag. Why they brought me to you is unknowable."

Without saying anything Excalibur cuts one of the vines with his machete, Julia screams in pain, "No you fucking idiot!" The vine stabs Excalibur in the chest, he screams and falls to his knees. The vine heals itself. "Excalibur, are you finally dead you bastard man?" Julia asks.

The gaping wound that exposed Excalibur's beating heart heals itself. He touches his chest, amazed and confused, "No, I'm not. How am I not fucking dead?"

"Damn, so it's true," she says.

"What?"

"The report we stole from Ouroboros all those years ago was filled with a lot of bullshit and misinformation. One of the things it said was that you drank the Waters Of Life from the Chalice Of Eternity. We also underestimated the incompetence of the military. If such a thing existed, they wouldn't destroy it in a fire, never underestimate how dumb and shitty people can be. Like I did with you. I should have paid attention to the warning signs.

"Why did you do it Excalibur?"

He says, "Back then I lied to Azucar. I told him it was some grand revenge plan that I did it for the Monkeys, Felicity, and Marco. That I was hoping for a better world shaped in my image." He wipes the tears from his eyes, "I did it for me Julia, I was deluding myself. I was angry and didn't care if I brought everyone down with me. I was hurting and felt like everyone had to pay for it."

The vines slither and shake, they plant themselves on the walls, and lift Julia above Excalibur. She yells, "Oh poor you! Were you a sad, angry little boy! Is that why all those people had to die, is that why you pushed everyone away, why you live in the middle of nowhere? Fuck you, you're a sad, pathetic piece of shit! We're both undying abominations that you created, the only difference is that I look like the monster I am.

"You worthless fucking coward, you think you can run from what you've done. That you can live a quiet life! Have you been to ground zero?"

"No." he says.

"No!" she yells.

"You're right" he says, "I should bear witness to what I've done. I can't outrun this forever." He climbs out of the well, the light is blinding.

He sells everything he owns to the guy who owns the general store and buys his old truck. The vines make Julia follow him. They get into the truck and start their trip to New York City. The drive is silent, neither of them say anything.

They're stopped at a checkpoint by an army of Russian soldiers, when they try to touch Julia the vines slaughter them. She cries and begs them to stop. The surviving soldiers let them through and give them a wide berth.

"Were those Russians?" Excalibur asks.

Still recovering from their slaughter, she takes a few moments to respond, "Jesus dude, you really don't know what you fucking did! Yea dude, you started a world war. With no one to blame, the US started pointing fingers, this set off a chain reaction nobody knew who to believe or who to side with. I don't even know who's at war with who anymore, it seems like the Russians change their allegiance every other month. Mostly the allegiances are out of convenience and what the countries can get. The world has been fractured and only a handful of big countries remain."

They stop to get gas and snacks. Everyone stares at her and takes pictures, the shutter clicks make her feel like an object to be gawked at. She begs them to keep their distance, a few of them don't, the vines wipe them away sending them flying. She apologies.

A massive concrete wall surrounds ground zero, it's so big that it blots out the midday sun and creates its own micro ecosystem. There's only one gate in and out of the city. Special operatives protect the gate, they can let people in but can't let people out. Surrounding the wall are millions of people, mourners, and people saying prayers for those who had no one when they died. The wall is covered in names etched into it.

Julia's vines lift Excalibur so he can the city. They reach so high and cause such a scene that there's complete silence for a few moments as everyone watches in amazement.

The giants of the city are reduced to hollow shells. Metal structures that once towered over millions of people are now metal beams falling into each other. A thick layer of brown dust blankets the ground. There's a low hum, the smell of death still clings in the air after all these years. He stares at the devastation for several minutes before the vines lower him to the ground.

He stares at his feet hen jumps in his truck. The vines chase after him and jump on the truck. "Where are you going?" Julia yells. Excalibur says nothing.

He parks in front of a black ominous building, the only thing on the building are giant white letters that spell, News. Excalibur walks in with confidence and looks around until he finds the live broadcast room. There's a red blinking light above the door that indicates they're live. He walks in, steps in front of the camera and says, "Hello, I'm Excalibur and I dropped the nukes." A cop shoots him in the head. A few moments pass, he gets up, "I'm also undying, which sounds cool but fucking sucks! Am I allowed to say that on TV? I'm sorry."

A dozen men dressed in black swarm him. The news cast applaud their masters.

They throw him in the back of windowless vans and take him to a concentration camp that's under construction.

One of the first things they ask him is, "Why would you go on national television and lie like that?" He tries to explain who he is and what he did, but they don't believe him.

"Please, I'm telling the truth!" he pleads.

"We'll see about that," one of them says. They inject him then say, "We found that torture doesn't really work. You people will say anything! So we made this truth serum, you can't lie, go ahead and try it should be working now."

"My name is Ph-Ph-Phil. My name is Excalibur!"

"Ah, excellent. Now did you drop the bombs?"

"Yes!"

His captors look at each other with shock, "Where did you fire them from?" One of them asks.

"Area ninety-nine." He says.

A lady dressed all in blue comes in. She looks at Excalibur strapped to the chair, she grins, and with a malicious tinge says, "My god it's really you."

Part 6: Space Oddity

On every national news channel in every country, Excalibur is tortured and questioned for hours by multiple state agencies from different countries. They kill him just to see him come back to life multiple times.

Every nation in the world comes together to hate Excalibur. The longest period of peace in history is achieved. After days of talks, the nations of the world come together to develop a spaceship that can fly in one direction forever. With their efforts combined, this takes a year.

Excalibur is strapped in the generational ship, his expulsion from the planet is watched by billions. Every angle physically possible if filmed there's even a camera a few feet from his faces so they can all watch his terrified screams.

The earth shakes as the massive generational ship blasts off into the great inky sky toward the Andromeda galaxy. The world leaders shake hands on a job well done. This world peace is maintained for another few hours.

Excalibur flies past the moon, and the straps are released. He floats to a window with a view of the earth and stares at it until it becomes a blip of light. A few earth days pass before he falls asleep, the perfect well light glow of his prison is horrifying. He looks around the ship for food but finds nothing, the only living thing on board is himself.

Days pass and he gets hungry. Months pass, he starves but doesn't die. The constant gnawing of dehydration is also getting to him. He cuts off his leg then eats it, the pain, horror, and complications that come with doing this make it not worth doing again. He tries to find water but the faucets and pipes aren't connected to anything; he looks at the space under the cabinet where piping would be and finds empty space.

The only form of entertainment he has in the ship is a room filled with books in languages he doesn't speak. The only books with English in them are translation guides, it takes Excalibur several months of looking through every book to realize this.

Time loses all meaning for him, he pours over translation guides and language textbooks for weeks at a time. Years pass him by, the only thing he has to indicate change is the length of his beard. He watches himself turn into a skeletal man with a long flowing beard; he watches himself grow older. When he stops aging at fifty, he thinks he's finally lost his mind.

Decades, then centuries past. His beard gets longer and longer, filling the ship. He learns every language and reads every book he has multiple times. He tries to write his own novels but finds the only thing he can think to write about is a man who's trapped in a boat at sea. So he does, for decades he does nothing but write these books, before he knows it he's written the longest single work of fiction in all the galaxies.

His mind breaks, he retreats inward. Creating his own world, he dreams. Drowning in his own beard, he drifts endlessly.

Made in the USA
Monee, IL
13 June 2022